"Why don't you get some rest?"

It was against Savannah's nature to leave things undone. She desperately needed order of some sort. "The dishes—"

"I'll do them."

Whether Sam Walters had intended this or not, she didn't feel quite as alone anymore. She felt...things perhaps she shouldn't. Especially given the circumstances. But there was something about the gentleness beneath his brash exterior, the kindness he extended when she least expected it, that broke through all her barriers, filling the heart she'd been so sure was now just an empty shell.

The man did dishes, for heaven's sake. And there was something in his smile. Something reassuring and...

"You're a rare man, Sam Walters." In more ways than one, she added silently.

Dear Reader,

I'm always getting letters telling me how much you love miniseries, and this month we've got three great ones for you. Linda Turner starts the new family-based miniseries, THOSE MARRYING McBRIDES! with *The Lady's Man*. The McBrides have always been unlucky in love—until now. And it's wedding-wary Zeke who's the first to take the plunge. Marie Ferrarella also starts a new miniseries this month. CHILDFINDERS, INC. is a detective agency specializing in finding missing kids, and they've never failed to find one yet. So is it any wonder desperate Savannah King turns to investigator Sam Walters when her daughter disappears in *A Hero for All Seasons?* And don't miss *Rodeo Dad,* the continuation of Carla Cassidy's wonderful Western miniseries, MUSTANG, MONTANA.

Of course, that's not all we've got in store. Paula Detmer Riggs is famous for her ability to explore emotion and create characters who live in readers' minds long after the last page is turned. In *Once More a Family* she creates a reunion romance to haunt you. Sharon Mignerey is back with her second book, *His Tender Touch,* a suspenseful story of a woman on the run and her unwilling protector—who soon turns into her willing lover. Finally, welcome new author Candace Irvin, who debuts with a military romance called *For His Eyes Only.* I think you'll be as glad as we are that Candace has joined the Intimate Moments ranks.

Enjoy—and come back next month, when we once again bring you the best and most exciting romantic reading around.

Yours,

Leslie J. Wainger
Executive Senior Editor

Please address questions and book requests to:
Silhouette Reader Service
U.S.: 3010 Walden Ave., P.O. Box 1325, Buffalo, NY 14269
Canadian: P.O. Box 609, Fort Erie, Ont. L2A 5X3

MARIE FERRARELLA

A HERO FOR ALL SEASONS

Silhouette®

INTIMATE™ MOMENTS®

Published by Silhouette Books

America's Publisher of Contemporary Romance

To
Leslie Wainger,
For generosity
above
and beyond

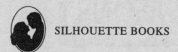 SILHOUETTE BOOKS

ISBN 0-373-07932-X

A HERO FOR ALL SEASONS

Copyright © 1999 by Marie Rydzynski-Ferrarella

This edition published by arrangement with Harlequin Books S.A.

® and TM are trademarks of Harlequin Books S.A., used under license.
Trademarks indicated with ® are registered in the United States Patent
and Trademark Office, the Canadian Trade Marks Office and in other
countries.

Look us up on-line at: http://www.romance.net

Printed in U.S.A.

MARIE FERRARELLA

lives in Southern California. She describes herself as the tired mother of two overenergetic children and the contented wife of one wonderful man. This RITA Award-winning author is thrilled to be following her dream of writing full-time.

Chapter 1

He knew her.

The minute Sam Walters looked up to see who Alex, the agency's secretary, had brought into his office, he knew her. Knew the tall, vivid-looking blonde who had come seeking his help—even before he actually recognized her and put a name to her face.

With the investigative agency almost a year, Sam nonetheless had more than a few years of law enforcement experience to fall back on. He was well acquainted with the aura of just barely controlled panic that he saw around the woman's mouth, with the edgy nervousness in her gait that was just a hair away from being visible and overpowering. And with the fear that was eating away at her and vying for possession of her soul.

He'd seen it all before, in every shade, every size. Victims who were struggling not to be.

Just the way Savannah King was.

He absorbed details as quickly, as unconsciously, as he breathed. It came that naturally to him.

She was a stunning woman by anyone's reckoning, but Sam still didn't miss the fact that Savannah King was pale beneath her suntan, pale and shaken.

But it was her eyes that caught his attention. There was something there, something within the crystal-blue eyes that spoke to Sam. That told him that she wasn't going to break down here in his sunny corner office, dissolving in a flood of tears the way so many others who'd come to ChildFinders, Inc. had done. Those people had recited their stories in the halting bits and hurried pieces that reflected the shards of their once orderly lives.

She had guts, he thought. He'd bet on it. It made his job easier.

On his feet now to greet her, Sam rounded the desk that always seemed to be in an eternal state of clutter.

"Hello," he said warmly, his hand out. Behind them Alex withdrew unobtrusively.

After a beat, the willowy blonde extended her hand to him. It felt icy against his flesh, even though it was the middle of August. That didn't surprise him.

Savannah pressed her lips together before allowing herself to utter a single word. This man before her—this tall, rugged-looking man with the quirky smile on his lips and the shock of dark blond hair dipping down just above his eyes and rubbing against the collar of his blue shirt—was her last hope.

Last hope.

The words felt as if they were digging into her chest. Branding her. She drew a long breath to dislodge the talons.

"I'm—"

Sam wrapped his fingers around her hand, a mute promise in the strong gesture. She might not fall to pieces here, he guessed, but she was close. Damn close.

"Savannah King," he completed for her.

Releasing her hand, he softly closed the door behind her and locked out the extraneous noise. Except for the soft *whoosh* of the air-conditioning system, the office became incredibly quiet.

"Yes, I know." For a split second, Sam studied her face. She looked just as classy in person as she had on the broadcast yesterday, and only a shade less composed. "I saw you on TV last night."

The TV. Her father had pulled strings and called in favors to make sure that the story wasn't just lost in the waves of sound bytes that crossed the air every night. An influential man, Perry King had gotten her prime air time on every news channel Southern California carried. She'd had less than three minutes to make her plea. To turn a stone heart into something human.

By eight this morning, she'd known that she hadn't succeeded.

Savannah nodded, slowly taking in a measured

breath and then letting it out again. Everything
seemed like such an effort now: putting one foot in
front of the other, trying to think, keeping herself col-
lected. She felt like a mouse, trapped in an over-
whelmingly huge maze, desperately searching for the
right door. Not to get out—but to find what had been
so brutally snatched away from her.

To find her child.

Despite all the help coming her way, Savannah had
never felt so completely alone in her life. Lost and
alone.

She tried to smile. Her mouth barely curved.
"Hopefully, you weren't the only one who saw me."

Sam knew exactly what she was saying. The three-
minute spot, carried on all the local networks at five
and then again at eleven, had been directed at the
person who had taken her four-year-old daughter, Aimee, from her. He'd watched the first segment,
wedged into the news between a human interest story
and a story about a narrowly avoided midair colli-
sion—immediately alerted because this was what he
did: he looked for missing children.

No, Sam amended silently, he *found* missing children. That was the difference. It was what they all
did at the agency. ChildFinders, Inc.'s unequaled
track record was their personal contribution to the
world. His, and Megan's and Cade's. Cade Townsend
was the heart of it. Without Cade, there would have
been no contribution. No agency.

Sam pulled out the chair that stood in front of his

desk, the indication clear. Savannah made no move toward it.

"Would you like to sit down?"

He noticed that she looked at the chair as if she hadn't noticed it before. He understood that, too. Only things that had some connection to her daughter's disappearance were probably filtering in. The rest existed somewhere just outside the perimeter, unnoted, unimportant.

"Yes, thank you."

The words came out in a whisper. Savannah felt drained and just this side of hopeless, although she was struggling not to give in to the feeling. She couldn't. Defeat meant losing Aimee. She was ready to die before she allowed that to happen.

But it was an effort not to collapse into the chair. An effort not to give in to the darkness that was hovering around the edges of her world these last five days. The sensation was appallingly new to her. Savannah wasn't the type to collapse; she was the type to forge ahead, no matter what. This was the greatest test she'd ever faced, a thousand times worse than the heartbreak she'd endured before.

Savannah tried to hang on to her spirit, her feeling that Aimee *would* be found, with fingers that were growing increasingly tired, increasingly lax.

Maybe it was superstitious—absurd even—but she had this terribly uneasy feeling that if she let go, she'd never be able to find Aimee. Somehow, some way, she *had* to find her.

Which was what had brought her here to Child-

Finders, Inc. An agency begun by a man who'd had his own son snatched out of his life.

Funny how things you read in passing turn out to be the very things you wind up bartering your soul on. She remembered reading about Cade Townsend three months ago—reading about him and feeling sorry for what he had to be going through.

And now *she* knew how *he* felt.

The sad irony of it was that Darin Townsend remained the only missing child ChildFinders had not been able to recover.

Savannah felt a flutter in the pit of her stomach.

Oh please, let them find Aimee. Let her be safe. I'll do anything, anything—just let her be safe.

Savannah turned to watch Sam as he came around to stand before her. He moved with a confidence that she found encouraging. No bravado, just confidence. And there was sympathy in his eyes. Not pity—sympathy. She couldn't have handled pity.

"I'm Sam Walters," he told her, realizing that the introduction had been interrupted. "And I'm familiar with your story."

His tone was soft, gentle. She'd struck him last night as an intelligent, well-educated woman. To talk down to her would be an insult, but he knew the value of kindness and patience, even though he did without them as a rule in his personal life. He didn't need them. Other people did. Especially victims.

Sam took a micro-tape recorder from his drawer and placed it on his desk. Cade's rule. Everything at the initial session was recorded. It saved time and avoided discrepancies.

''But just for the record—'' he moved the machine closer to her ''—why don't you tell me what happened in your own words?''

The slight click as he turned on the tape recorder on his desk echoed in her brain. Savannah drew herself together, to attempt to stay just ahead of the words she was going to recite. Words that had sharp points on every letter, every syllable. Words that told how her life had gone from being wonderful to abysmal in the space of a heartbeat.

An elbow on each arm of the chair, unconsciously seeking support, Savannah knotted her hands together. The tension she was experiencing had breadth and depth. Instinctively, Sam laid his hand on top of hers, just for a moment, the slight pressure conveying to her what words couldn't.

A covenant.

She looked at him, their eyes meeting in a frozen instant in time. He couldn't read anything there—not gratitude, not anger. It was the gate to a fortress that was sealed.

Drawing back his hand, Sam leaned a hip against his desk, waiting. She'd begin when she was ready. There was no sense rushing her.

Savannah took a deep breath. It didn't help. Nothing helped. Her lungs ached from the tears she refused to shed.

Tears were for mourning, and she wouldn't mourn. Aimee wasn't dead, she was alive. Her daughter was out there somewhere, and they were going to find her. No matter what it took.

Her lips felt dry as she pushed out the words that she'd already said so many times before. With effort, Savannah tried to keep the story fresh, for Walters's benefit. He had to see, to hear, something the others had not.

He *had* to.

Every word cost her.

"I was shopping with Aimee—"

"When?" he cut in. Despite the tape recorder, he was already making notes in his notebook. Writing it all down helped him remember. Helped him sort.

She looked at him as if he hadn't been paying attention, then realized that she hadn't mentioned the day.

"Thursday. Last Thursday." A hundred years ago. "I'd taken the day off from my work because I'd promised Aimee an outing." Why hadn't she broken it? There'd been so many other promises she'd been forced to break or temporarily bend—why couldn't this have been one of them? Aimee would still be with her if she had. "We were in Lenard's—I had stopped to get a new dress." She paused, upbraiding herself. There'd been no real need for a new dress. It had been purely a whim on her part. One she was paying dearly for. "I told Aimee if she behaved, we'd go to the toy store next. She loves stuffed animals."

She was babbling, Savannah thought. She could feel the tears welling up in her throat and pushed them back. She wasn't going to cry. She didn't want this man to think of her as some fragile woman, on the cusp of shattering. He'd use that as an excuse, and she would give him no excuses to use as a roadblock. He had to let her do what she wanted to do. He *had* to.

Savannah focused on steadying her pulse, on being coherent.

"My back was turned for a minute. Maybe ninety seconds," Savannah amended, trying very hard to be as specific as was humanly possible. It hadn't felt that long, but maybe it had been. She wasn't sure any longer. "It was just long enough to read the sizes on three tags—no more."

Just long enough to make the difference. The accusation beat a heavy tattoo in her brain.

"When I looked down to ask Aimee what she thought of the color—she loves being consulted—" A half smile played on her lips as she thought of the way Aimee tried so very hard to behave like a grown-up. And then the smile vanished. Just the way Aimee had. "When I looked down," Savannah repeated with effort, "Aimee wasn't there."

Sam saw the glint then, the almost imperceptible shimmer of tears gathering. He wanted to say something, to comfort her. But he knew that there was nothing to be said. All the words would sound empty to her. She must have heard them all before. So instead, he waited in silence for her to continue.

Savannah shifted in her seat, knowing there was no way she was going to get comfortable. Not until the ordeal was finally over.

"I didn't think anything of it at first. Aimee has a weakness for climbing into circular racks of clothes and popping up in the middle, giggling. Drives the saleswomen crazy. I've told her not to, but…'' Her voice trailed off.

And then, raising her chin, Savannah rallied right in front of his eyes.

Sam had the distinct impression that he was watching Joan of Arc trying not to think of the straw pyre standing just outside her cell door.

Savannah concentrated on reciting the series of events in the order they occurred. Whether her heart was breaking ultimately made no difference in finding Aimee.

"I looked everywhere for her. The two saleswomen in the department helped me search. One of them called security. We couldn't find her.'' She'd felt so brittle, so fragile, calling Aimee's name over and over again, trying not to even remotely entertain the thought that someone had purposely taken her little girl.

But in the end, there was nothing else she could think.

Her voice deadened. "The police were called in half an hour later.''

Half an hour. The difference between finding a child and not. Sam closed the spiral pad. Every second counted against them. And now it was five long days later.

Sam kept his thoughts from his face as he nodded. "Do you have a photograph of Aimee with you?'' It was a rhetorical question to keep things moving. She'd stopped talking.

Savannah wanted to snap at him. To ask him what kind of a mother he thought she was—not to have a photograph of her child with her.

But there was an answer for that. She was the kind of mother who lost her child in a department store. She had no right to snap at anyone.

Savannah's hand shook as she took out her wallet. She was consumed with a rage, with a desire to hit something, to vent and scream. It wouldn't do any good, but at least she could discharge some of these feelings that were bouncing around inside her, clawing away at every inch of her.

Sam pretended not to notice the slight tremor in her hand as he accepted the photograph from her. There had been a photograph flashed on the screen along with the broadcast, but he wanted to study the child's features himself.

She was a beautiful child. A blond like her mother, the little girl's lively smile immediately jumped out at him. She was a child to notice, not to overlook. The kind that modeling agencies catering to television commercials prayed for. That all worked in their favor, he thought.

He placed the photograph on his desk beside the tape recorder. "May I keep this?" Savannah nodded stiffly. "Would you like something to drink? It's kind of hot today."

The air-conditioning was doing more than an adequate job of keeping the office cool, but he thought she needed to have something to do with her hands. To steady them. Sam moved toward the door, opening it.

No, I don't want anything to drink. I want my daughter back. I want my life back. Savannah bit back the edgy retort, and just shook her head.

"No, I'm fine." The irony of the words struck her instantly, and she laughed. It was a hollow, raspy sound. When he turned to look at her quizzically, she merely shook her head at the unwitting phrasing. "No, I'm not," she amended firmly. Her voice grew more steady, steely, even as she opened up this tiny window into the chaos her world had turned into. "I am *not* fine. I'm going out of my mind, Mr. Walters." She couldn't remain seated any longer. She rose and began pacing through the sunny office, but she saw only darkness. "I can't eat, I can't sleep, I keep going around in circles, forgetting what I'm supposed to be doing."

Of the three of them in the agency—if he didn't count Alex, who worked part-time—Sam was the best at putting people at their ease. But he felt as if he was out of his element here. Still, he had to say something. He had the feeling that he was at a missile site three minutes before liftoff. A disastrous liftoff.

"That's perfectly normal, Mrs. King—" he began to assure her.

Fairly or unfairly, Savannah lashed out at the patience she heard in his voice. She didn't want patience, or sympathy or any one of a myriad of emotions she'd been accosted with and tendered in the last one hundred twenty-one endless hours.

She wanted action.

Results.

Most of all, she wanted this to be over, and Aimee to be in her arms again.

"No, it's not normal," she contradicted vehemently. "It's hell. My own personal hell, and I want out of it." Her eyes leveled on his. She knew she was taking out her frustrations on him and he didn't deserve it, but she couldn't help herself. Once started, she couldn't stop herself. "I want my daughter and I will do anything, *anything,* to find her. Do you understand?"

Maybe he'd been wrong, Sam thought. Maybe she was going to break down. He wondered if Megan had returned. Sometimes the sympathy of another woman helped. Or maybe Alex could come in....

"I understand—"

No, he didn't. She turned on her heel. She'd heard so many platitudes and pat phrases these last five days. People who meant well, people who told her to hang in there and then went on with their undisturbed lives while she was looking at the shattered, jagged edges of her own. She'd had it with platitudes.

"Do you? Do you really? Forgive me, but until you've been through it, you can't possibly understand." She looked toward the door, as if expecting someone to materialize. "I asked for Mr. Townsend—"

Everybody did when they first called the agency.

Cade was the one who'd started the agency, the one the story was built around. But even Cade couldn't be everywhere at once. That was why he and Megan Andreini were around.

"I'm afraid he's not available right now. He's working on a case at the moment." Sam's eyes met hers. "I don't think you want to wait."

No, she didn't want to wait. She *couldn't* wait. Not if she was to remain in her own skin. Not if she was going to find Aimee.

Savannah dragged a shaky hand through her hair. Straight, long blond strands rained back into place on either side of her drawn face. She was taking it out on Walters, and he was only trying to help. Embarrassed, Savannah flushed, although she still couldn't quite muster a smile.

"I'm sorry."

A slight movement of his fingers waved the apology away.

"It's all right. No one expects you to be at your best at a time like this." Crossing to the door, Sam opened the door and signaled to Alex.

Looking up, the secretary nodded in response. Over the last few months, they'd worked out a code. She knew what Sam wanted.

Alex had a glass of lemonade in Sam's hand in less than three minutes.

"You're a treasure, Alex," he told her as she went back to her desk. Alex flashed him a smile, her fingers already flying over the keyboard.

Sam eased the door shut again, then crossed back

to Savannah. "What do you expect us to do that the police haven't?"

It was always best to have things up front and clear. People came to them because ChildFinders had a perfect recovery record—save for one. But with that reputation came the burden of waiting for the record to stop spinning, for the streak to be broken. He and Cade and Megan weren't magicians; they were only people. Dedicated people, but people nonetheless. People failed sometimes.

Gently, he slipped the glass between her hands, then closed her fingers around it.

Savannah accepted the lemonade. Moving on automatic pilot, she brought the rim of the glass to her lips and sipped, then looked at him pointedly.

A miracle.

That was what she wanted from them, pure and simple. She wanted them to perform a miracle, to do whatever it took to bring Aimee back to her.

Savannah set the glass down on the edge of the desk and looked up at Sam. Her voice was low, her demand urgent, unshakable.

"I want you to find Aimee."

Simple enough words, he thought. It was the responsibility that was enormous. He prodded her a little further. He'd been a policeman, and he knew how sensitive toes could be.

"You don't think the police are handling it correctly?"

It was a routine question that Sam asked at the beginning of each investigation. He needed to know the kind of person Savannah King was—the kind of person he was dealing with—before he undertook the case and all that it would entail. Not only her response, but her tone was important here. Everything provided input for him—clues, which in turn were all pieces of the puzzle he needed to put together before he made his first phone call.

There were times—more times than he cared to think about—when parents were responsible for their own children's disappearance. They put on a show to divert suspicion away from themselves. He had to be sure that he wasn't being duped, although if he were any judge of character, Sam had a gut feeling that Savannah King was on the level.

Either that, or one hell of an actress.

"It's not a matter of the police not doing their job correctly," she told him. She knew the odds. "Aimee's not the only child who's missing, not the only case they have to go on. This happened in Newport Beach." And the city was a large one, not quite as removed from crime as the city she lived in. Bedford was located only seven miles away, yet it was still young, still innocent. Still untouched by the kinds of things that ate away at older cities. "I want someone working for me. Exclusively. Someone whose only concern is finding Aimee, not half a dozen ongoing investigations and currently unsolved crimes."

She'd worded it diplomatically, he thought, a smile rising to his lips. That meant devastation hadn't won out over her control. He'd been right in his initial assessment.

She'd also given him the right reason, without hysteria. It was a good sign.

Sam nodded. "All right."

He made a judgment call. He accepted the case for the agency without first consulting Cade. If he were being honest with himself, he'd accepted the case—at least in theory—the moment he'd seen Savannah on the news yesterday. Her impassioned plea to the kidnapper had gotten to him, despite the fact that he'd tried over the months to anesthetize himself to a degree when it came to his cases.

He didn't want to get too close. Being too close, Cade had told him when he joined the agency, robbed you of your edge and your objectivity. Cade was right on the money with that one.

But then, Sam had already learned that lesson a long time ago, on a more personal basis.

The smile he gave her was encouraging. "We'll take your case, Mrs. King."

"It's Miss King," she corrected flatly.

There were no feelings behind the words. Whatever she had felt for Jarred had died a long time ago. There were, however, feelings behind the next thing she said. A wealth of feelings.

"Thank you. And there is one more thing..." Savannah added.

Sam waited, wondering where this addendum was going. "Yes?"

"I want to be part of the investigation."

Chapter 2

The request hung between them, framed in silence, as Sam looked at Savannah. He had an uneasy feeling that there was a great deal more to it than appeared on the surface.

Maybe it was just paranoia, catching up to him.

After all, the request was a perfectly logical one. He could understand her need to know what he was doing on her behalf at all times. If he knew the police, they had undoubtedly shut her out. There was neither time nor energy to hold a victim's hand. Everything was focused on solving the crime.

While understandable, it was frustrating to the victim, especially with a crime like this. He'd come to realize that this past year.

Sam laid a comforting hand on her shoulder. "Of course we'll keep you apprised as much as possible."

Savannah shrugged his hand away before she could think better of it. She hadn't meant to be rude; it was just that right now everything made her feel so boxed in.

"Not apprised," she corrected. "Abreast."

She had absolutely no intention of being shut out or pushed to the sidelines. Not again. Especially not if she was paying for the investigation. She needed to *know,* to be *doing* something to help find her daughter. The endless minutes that crammed themselves into this agonizing business of waiting were driving her crazy.

She couldn't mean what he thought she meant. "Excuse me?"

Savannah struggled not to make her words sound like a demand. He didn't look like a man who responded well to demands. But she felt like demanding. Everyone was treating her like a fragile cut-glass vase—unable to think, to function. Unable to contribute. She desperately needed to contribute, to feel useful. If she didn't do something soon, she was afraid she was going to fall apart.

"I want to be there with you." Her eyes met his. "Every step of the way."

She meant it, too, he realized.

Just what he needed: having her second-guess him and create twice as much work. He didn't want to put her off, but he certainly didn't want her glued to his side during the investigation, either.

Sam tried to word his refusal as tactfully as possible. The lady had been through a lot. "I'm afraid that's not the way we work."

And even if it were, it wasn't the way he worked. Without his consciously making an effort or planning it, there was a distinct separation between the personality Sam turned toward the public, and the one he assumed with the people he interacted with when he was on the job. On an investigation, the amiable, friendly demeanor most of the world saw was sublimated. His actions and thoughts became exceedingly focused, exceedingly streamlined. His manner was sharp, at times abrupt. And at all times, he was in control and forceful. Someone coming along would only get in his way.

And a distraught mother—no matter how easy on the eye she was—would definitely get in his way.

He'd always moved better alone. Which was probably why, at the age of thirty-one, aside from his siblings' families, he still was alone.

Sam's answer was unacceptable. Savannah's eyes narrowed.

"One of the reasons I came here was because I need someone looking for Aimee who isn't bound up by rules and protocol. I need someone who can get dirty, if that's what's necessary." She looked at his eyes. They understood each other, at least about that. Whatever it took, that's what she wanted. The only rights that concerned her were Aimee's. "I need to have someone in my corner, working for me."

So far, they were in sync, and he meant to keep it that way.

"I understand that, and I will be working for you. That doesn't necessarily mean doing everything you ask," he emphasized. She didn't like what he was saying—he could see it. Sam tried to clarify his position. "What you are buying, Ms. King, is our combined expertise. You're paying us to do the job the best way we see fit—not the way you tell us to. There *is* a difference," he said pointedly. "If there's a conflict there, we'll go with the proven way every time. We *want* to find your daughter," he stressed.

"But—"

"Now I know this is hard for you, but just let me do my job the way I work best. All right?" He looked into her eyes, and moved out on that limb he knew he had no business being on. But the look, the sadness, in her eyes gave him no choice. "I promise I'll find your little girl for you."

He had nothing concrete to base his promise on. She knew that. But reason and common sense took a back seat to emotional neediness. She was desperate to find something to cling to.

She clung to his words.

For now, because he seemed unmovable, she withdrew her plea. They'd try it his way. Maybe it would work better in the long run.

Maybe, Savannah prayed, if she was very, very good, and cooperated, Aimee would be in her arms by tomorrow.

She took a deep breath, her eyes never leaving his. If he didn't believe what he had just said to her, she felt confident that she would have sensed it. He believed he could find Aimee. So she believed, too.

"All right."

Sam smiled at her. She was going to be reasonable. They weren't going to waste time with that. He got down to business.

"What's the name of the police detective who's handling your case?"

Was he going to duplicate the information that had already been gathered? It felt as if suspicions were waiting to assault her at every corner. "Why, is that important?"

It was very important, but it served no purpose to get into chapter and verse with her. Sam gave her an abbreviated answer.

"I don't like stepping on toes any more than I have to. As a rule, the police are not crazy about private investigators." He knew he hadn't been, when he was on the force. A great many P.I.s impeded investigations rather than aided in them.

That sounded like rivalry to her. "Aren't you all working toward a single goal?"

It was a reasonable enough assessment on the surface. In a perfect world, there would be no need to worry about thin-skinned police detectives. Everyone would just pool their information.

But the world was far from perfect. "Yes, but each team wants to be the one that scores the winning run." There was competition between the departments, between agencies. It was a fact of life.

Sam knew of several police detectives who considered him a traitor for having left the force, and who would rather see him drawn and quartered than share the time of day—much less information—with him. At the very least, he needed to know who was heading the investigation on this one.

Sam's metaphor must have registered on the perimeter of her mind. A light came into her eyes as she remembered. ''Baseball fan'?''

There'd been a time he'd been rabid about it. But that seemed as if it belonged to another lifetime, maybe even another person. When he'd had an actual life.

Still, he was fond of the sport. ''Whenever I get a chance to go.'' Usually, it was to take one of his nephews to a home game.

Savannah's father had been an enthusiast in his time. She'd gone for the hot dogs, and to keep him company. Back when she had still thought that she could bond with him. Memories nudged at one another. The world had seemed so much simpler then.

Savannah squeezed her eyes shut, pushing back the threat of tears.

''Aimee loves the Angels. She thinks they're real ones. She always asks if they're going to be wearing their wings to the game.'' Savannah blew out a breath, reeling in control again. For one second, she thought she'd lost her grip on it. She raised her eyes to his. He was still waiting. ''His name's Detective Ben Underwood.''

Underwood. The familiar name set him at ease.

Sam had gone through the academy with Underwood and his cousin Mike.

"Good guy," he assured her. Underwood was thorough, if a little short in the people skills. "Knows his stuff." Rounding his desk, Sam sat down and pulled over his notebook. "Okay, we're going to get to work now. I'm going to have to ask you a whole barrage of questions." He wondered if she was up to it. If he didn't miss his guess, her edges looked as if they were becoming a little frayed. "You have time?"

Every moment passed like a fly with its wings dipped in glue. "I have nothing *but* time, Mr. Walters." Still feeling agitated, she sat down again, perching on the edge of the chair.

"It's Sam," he told her. "Just Sam. Then let's get started." The sooner he got this out of the way, the sooner he could begin trying to put the pieces together.

But as he picked up his pen, the telephone rang. Sam frowned at it. Alex knew better than to let a call come through when he was with a client. He wondered why she'd let this slip by. When the telephone rang again, Sam stopped the tape recorder.

"Excuse me a minute." Picking up the receiver, he immediately began talking. "Alex, I'm a little busy right now."

The secretary's soft Southern lilt filled his ear. "Yes, I know, Sam, but he said it was an emergency."

Sam heard the smile in Alex's voice. "'He'?"

"Joey."

Sam sighed, then flashed an apologetic look toward Savannah as he held up his index finger. He had to take this call.

"This'll only take a minute," he promised. "Put him through, Alex."

The next moment, he heard the childish voice of his godson: his brother Terry's youngest son. "Hi, Uncle Sam."

A giggle followed the salutation. It always did. At six, Joey was still tickled by the fact that his very favorite uncle in the whole world could be addressed the same way as the venerable old symbol for the country in which he lived.

Joey knew all about Uncle Sam because Sam had made a point of telling him. Sam loved Joey's exuberance and innocent joy. But right now, it was intruding.

Turning his chair away from Savannah and toward the window, Sam lowered his voice. "Joey, I'm in the middle of something. I'll have to call you back."

Joey seemed not to hear. Like an arrow, he went straight to the target on which his mind was fixed. "Are you going to come to my party a week from next Saturday? It's my birthday and Mom says I can have anyone I want. I want you."

The declaration warmed his heart. There wasn't anything purer than the love of a child. He'd always believed that. Sam felt he was one of the lucky ones. He had no children of his own, but he enjoyed a unique relationship with his nephew. With all his nephews, in fact, as well as his niece. The only unmarried one in the family, Sam could afford to lavish both time and gifts on the children the way their parents couldn't.

He knew exactly how he'd feel if someone snatched Joey away from him. Just the way the woman in his office was feeling.

"Hey, I know it's your birthday. Wouldn't miss it for the world, partner, but right now I have to help a nice lady find her little girl. I'll talk to you later."

"Okay. Good luck," Joey added as an afterthought. His dad had told him what Uncle Sam did for a living, and Joey was very proud of him. "If anyone can find her, you can. 'Bye."

Here's hoping you're right, Joey, Sam thought, replacing the receiver in the cradle. He moved the chair around again.

"Sorry about that."

She'd heard the love in Sam's voice, the patience when he'd spoken to the child. It made her feel a little more secure in her belief. "Your son?"

He laughed as he shook his head. Sam glanced at the framed eight-by-ten on his desk. It was a photograph taken of the whole family at Big Bear last year. His arm was hooked around Joey's waist. Joey was laughing. "My nephew."

That impressed her even more. The man's extended family felt free to call him. He understood children. She couldn't put into words why that was so important to her, but that didn't diminish the fact that it was.

"How old is he?"

"Joey's going to be seven in two weeks." Even as he told her, Sam could hardly believe it. It seemed only the other day that Terry was telling him Gina was pregnant again. "I was just getting an invitation to his party," he explained, nodding at the telephone. A smile played on his lips as he remembered something Joey had said to him. "According to his friends, I bring 'the coolest gifts.'" Sam stopped abruptly as he realized he'd allowed himself to stray into a private area. That wasn't why she was here. "I'm sorry, this must be hard for you."

That was putting it mildly, she thought, but she had enjoyed hearing the one-sided exchange. For one moment, it made her feel almost normal again. Almost.

"Everything is hard for me, Sam," she admitted. "But at least I know you're the right man for the job."

He didn't ask her what brought her to that conclusion. It was enough that she'd reached it. "I wouldn't be sitting here in this chair if I wasn't." He pressed the record button again on the tape recorder. "Let's get to work."

Savannah liked the sound of that. Liked, too, the feeling that fleetingly passed through her. The feeling that she was doing something beyond just staring at the walls, holding her breath. Something beyond praying and making deals with a God she was no longer sure was listening.

She moved forward in her seat, eager to do anything that might help.

Though none of what he had to ask her to relive

was going to be easy, Sam knew that this might very well be the most awkward section. He wanted to get it out of the way first.

He watched her carefully for any telltale reactions. "Before we explore any other avenues, I have to ask this." She stiffened slightly, and he wondered what she was bracing for. "Is there any chance that Aimee's natural father might have taken her?" Savannah opened her mouth, and he was quick to stop her. "Think carefully," he cautioned. "Was there anything he might have said or done the last time you spoke that—"

She held up her hand to stop him. There was no need for Sam to go down that alley. There was only a dead end waiting.

"I don't have to think carefully. Aimee's father is in England right now." *Aimee's father.* She didn't think of him that way. Not even in the beginning. Jarred was more like the donor she'd inadvertently gone to to create something exquisitely wonderful. "He's been living there for the last four years."

She could see by the look in his eyes that distance wasn't enough to convince Sam that Jarred was out of the picture. Sam obviously needed more.

Savannah dug deep, giving him a piece of herself that she never shared. This was for Aimee.

"The affair was very passionate, very satisfying and very quick—at least on his part." She, on the other hand, had taken longer to get over him. But she'd managed. A disparaging smile twisted her lips. "Like the old song goes, it was too hot not to cool down. I just didn't realize it." But that was because she'd believed in love once. Believed with all her heart. The same heart Jarred crumbled. Jarred had been her teacher. In more ways than one.

Savannah looked at Sam. She hated talking about this. It made her feel so vulnerable. She supposed that at the time, she had been. But it was different now. Her heart was her own, and it only belonged to Aimee.

"The affair was over long before Aimee was born. He didn't even know I was pregnant."

Sam found himself wondering how a man could walk away of his own accord from someone like Savannah King. She didn't seem like the type of woman who would come along every day.

"Didn't you tell him when you found out?"

His question took her back over the years. She'd thought about it. Long and hard. It had been her first impulse when she'd found out, but she'd forced herself to put down the telephone. Those weren't the terms on which she wanted Jarred back in her life. She wanted him to return because he loved her—not because he felt bound to "do the right thing."

"No. I didn't want to make it seem as if I were using pregnancy to get him back." But in the interest of fairness, she had to let him know he had a child, a beautiful, blue-eyed smiling daughter. "I did, however, send him a birth announcement when she was born."

Savannah stared straight ahead, looking out the agency's first-floor window, knowing if she saw the least shred of sympathy in Sam's eyes, she would get up and walk out. And she didn't have the luxury of taking that option.

So she looked past his head, watching a seagull— less than a mile from the ocean—soar on a current of air.

Even now, what she told him next hurt to admit. "He sent a savings bond in the return mail. A very generous one." Though she tried to filter it out, a note of bitterness seeped into her voice. Not for herself, but for Aimee. "No note, no inquiry."

"No denial?" Some of the guys he'd known when he was in his early twenties would have been quick to deny any paternal responsibility.

With regal calm, Savannah turned her eyes to his. "He knew Aimee was his."

She didn't bother adding that Aimee's father had been her first love and her first lover. It seemed so hopelessly old-fashioned to admit to that. Besides, that was no business of his. Knowing that wouldn't help him find Aimee.

"And you've had no contact with him since then?" Sam probed.

Though it happened every day, Sam personally found that difficult to believe. How could you have a child and never try to get in contact with him or her? Never want to know how that child was doing, or even if he or she was well? He just didn't understand people like that.

She pressed her lips together. How many ways was he going to explore this? "None."

Sam drew a line through the top sentence. That ruled out parental abduction.

And made the possibilities a little more gritty—a little less safe, he thought grimly.

Sam went on to his next questions.

Two hours later, Sam was at the outdoor mall, retracing the steps Savannah had told him she'd taken that day that would forever be burned into her memory.

Savannah had looked drained when she left his office, Sam thought. She'd told him that she was going to her parents' house. Calling in another favor, her father had gotten an 800 number set up yesterday morning to field the calls they'd all hoped would come in after her appearance on the news. She told him the calls had come in far greater numbers than they'd ever expected. Her parents, sister and several of her friends from work were right now manning the lines set up in her parents' house.

Experience told Sam that the calls that were coming in would probably all lead nowhere, but he refrained from saying so to her. You never knew. Telecasts had occasionally been responsible for the capture of criminals. He'd learned early on that no stone should ever be left unturned, no possibility unexplored.

Maybe his job would be done before it was even started.

But he doubted it.

As she was leaving, Savannah had given him her

cell-phone number, and asked him to call immediately if he thought he found anything that might give her hope.

She'd flushed a little as she said it, and he remembered thinking that it made her look as if she were barely out of her teens, instead of a woman who had just entered her third decade.

"I know I must sound as if I'm begging—"

"You sound," he'd cut in, "like a concerned mother. I'll call," he promised.

But he wasn't going to, he thought—not if he didn't have anything to tell her. So far, he wasn't turning up anything that might be helpful, other than a theory he was playing with.

He'd gone back to Lenard's and shown Aimee's photograph to everyone he could find associated with the department store. Some of the clerks were eager to help; others, after being subjected to police questioning, had already become tired of the ordeal.

He talked to the pushcart vendors next. But no one had seen anything unusual prior to the police's arrival. Questioning one vendor after another, Sam came up with the same answers. There'd been no one who stood out, no man or woman tugging on a child's arm, or trying to drag a child who fit Aimee's description away. Nothing noteworthy to break the monotony of a Thursday morning until the police had shown up.

Sam was down to his last vendor when an idea struck him. He pocketed Aimee's photograph. "How about a little boy around that height?" Sam asked the man.

The vendor, a man far more interested in pushing overpriced hot dogs onto a hungry lunch crowd, looked at him in confusion as he speared the last order and set it comfortably onto a bun. "I thought you said you were looking for a little girl."

Was that a glint he saw in the vendor's eyes? Sam pressed on.

"Whoever took her didn't necessarily have to be clumsy about it. He or she—or they—might have thought to disguise the little girl before they took off with her." He'd struck a nerve, Sam thought. The man was now paying more than passing attention to him. "It's possible that they took her into the bathroom and changed her clothes, stuck her hair under a cap. At that age, it's not hard to disguise gender."

Plunging his arm into a sea of ice, the man dug deep for the can of cola that had just been requested by his customer. He grinned at Sam over his shoulder. "Hey, that's pretty clever."

"Yeah, clever." From where Sam stood, it was pretty disgusting. It took all kinds. Still hoping to be on to something, Sam continued to press. "Did you see a boy being dragged away?"

Quickly, pushing change into his customer's hand, the vendor lost no time in taking out a small, battered notepad he kept tucked in his back pocket. He scribbled a note to himself that looked more like one continuous wavy line.

"No, but I can use the idea for this screenplay I'm working on." A grin split his face. "This is just my day job. My agent says—"

But Sam didn't have time to listen to what the man's agent said.

"Here." Sam pressed his business card into the hot-dog vendor's hand. "If you remember anything, or hear anything—" after all, the vendors did talk and maybe he'd missed one today "—call me."

The vendor read the name on the card. "Child-Finders, Inc. Pretty catchy." He turned the card around between his forefinger and thumb, obviously thinking. "Got a patent on that?"

"Yeah, we got a patent on it." Sam had no idea whether Cade did or not, but he wasn't about to waste any more time discussing it.

Sam walked away quickly, before he told the man what he could do with his screenplay, his agent and, for that matter, his pushcart full of overpriced hot dogs.

Chapter 3

"**Y**ou look like hell."

The voice, low and smooth like fine old scotch being poured over ice, pushed its way into Sam's consciousness and mingled with the notes he was reviewing on his desk. Notes that had begun to merge and scramble, telling him he needed to take a break.

Sam looked up, surprised that daylight had managed to covertly slip into the office to usurp the dark. He was even more surprised that he was no longer alone in the office. Megan and Cade had walked in without his even being aware of it.

So much for being in the running for the title of Supercop of the Year, Sam thought sarcastically. "Thanks," he muttered. "Nice to see you, too."

Sam caught his reflection in the window. If anything, Megan's assessment had been kind. He could do with some sleep, and then a shower and shave. Fresh clothes wouldn't hurt, either.

He straightened, rotating his shoulders slowly. There was a dull ache between the blades.

Pausing, Cade set his motorcycle helmet down on the edge of Sam's desk and eyed Sam's rumpled appearance. After having Sam at the agency for almost a year, he was well acquainted with the signs by now. "You on a new case?"

The question caught Sam off guard. "What?" And then he remembered. He'd skipped a step in procedure. "Oh, yeah, I am. Sorry."

Cade was lax about rules, but he did want to be notified whenever a new case came into the office. Sam knew he should have at least left a note on Cade's desk, but paperwork had never been his forte. He always managed to put it off. It was one of the reasons he'd left the force. But not the main one.

He tried to make amends now. "Client's name is Savannah King."

The name immediately rang a bell for both Megan and Cade.

"The woman on the news the other night?" Megan asked. She took a sip from her huge container of espresso, then frowned thoughtfully. "The case isn't very old." This was Tuesday. Megan would have expected the family to have allowed the police a little more time.

"Ten minutes is a long time if it's your child who's been abducted."

The remark might just have been a casual observation, had it not been Cade who said it. Even now, more than two years later, he still worked every case with one eye toward uncovering a link between the case and his own son's abduction.

Megan silently upbraided herself for the slip. She should have known better. She'd first met Cade when she'd been called in as one of the team of FBI special agents assigned to handle his son's kidnapping. Kidnapping cases had been her field of expertise ever since she'd first joined the Bureau. It was by request. She had the background for it. When she was ten years old, her older brother had been kidnapped from in front of their house. Chad lived with their mother. It was five years before the case was finally solved. Five years before she'd discovered that it had been her own father, estranged from her mother, who had taken Chad. That gave Megan the unique perspective of being personally acquainted with the hell that both the family of the victim and the family of the abductor endured. It also gave her her mission in life—to help reunite as many abducted children with their families as possible. When circumstances had arranged themselves to tie her hands at the Bureau, she'd left. It turned out to be a fortuitous move. Joining Cade's agency allowed her far more leeway to accomplish her goal.

"Sorry," she murmured. She wouldn't cause Cade any pain for the world.

Cade laid a hand on her shoulder, mutely absolving her of any guilt pangs. He wore his pain stoically and silently. It was easy at times for others to forget that he was still among the walking wounded.

Nodding, Cade looked at the clutter of paper on Sam's desk. Sam had a tendency to burn the midnight oil when he was working on a case. He respected that. "Getting anywhere with it?"

Sam gathered some of the stray pages together, but before he could answer, Megan pressed the large container of espresso into his hands. "Here, I think you need this more than I do."

Right about now, he would have killed for a cup of coffee. Grateful, Sam took a long sip. When he finally spoke, his voice was raspy.

"How can you drink this stuff?" He pushed the cup away from him.

Megan reached for it and took a large swallow. "Keeps me hopping."

"More like bouncing off the walls."

He turned toward Cade and answered the man's question. "All I've done is just gone over the stuff everyone already knows." It had been a long, tedious exercise in futility, but he liked having everything organized, at least in his own mind.

After leaving the mall, Sam had gone to the local branch office of the L.A. newspaper. He knew one of the editors there, and that had gotten him into the current back issues with a minimum of effort. He'd read everything he could on the case, making copies for himself before going to see Ben Underwood.

But the detective wasn't in the office, so Sam had to settle for a few inside, off-the-record observations made by one of the patrolmen who had been the first on the scene. All of it had added up to very little.

"There was an 800 number flashing on the bottom of the screen during her plea," Cade recalled. "Did you get the telephone records of the calls that came in yet?"

"On my list of things to do," Sam replied. Sam grinned at the man he had come to respect a great deal. "Not all of us are superhuman."

"Work on it," Cade said, his expression deadpan as he picked up the papers Sam had been jotting notes on and skimmed them quickly. He tried to recall what he'd heard on the news about the King kidnapping.

One thing jumped out at him. "No ransom note?"

Sam set his mouth grimly. "None."

They all knew what that meant. It didn't bode well. Still, there might be other options. "No relative lurking in the shadows?"

"None so far."

Tired, punchy, Sam tried to keep the frustration he felt out of his voice. He should have sacked out on the sofa and caught a couple of hours of sleep. But he'd gotten caught up, the way he always did, and had wanted to get things organized as quickly as possible.

"How about a disgruntled housekeeper or babysitter? Someone nursing a grudge, or overly attached to the little girl?" Megan suggested. She avoided mentioning other possibilities. None of them liked thinking about the darker alternatives to a kidnapping for ransom.

Sam raised his eyes to Megan, watching her drain the last of what tasted, if he were being kind, like hot ashes to him from her container. "Trying to tell me how to do my job? I realize that I'm still the rookie here compared to you two, but—"

After flipping the empty container into his trash basket, Megan kissed the top of Sam's head. She'd been the one who had brought him to Cade in the first place when Sam had expressed dissatisfaction with his career. Their friendship went back more than thirteen years, to the second row in ninth-grade geometry. Back then, Sam had only been a little taller than she was. Now, more than a foot separated them.

She laughed at his disgruntled expression. "Touchy, touchy."

Sam waved a disparaging hand toward the waste basket. "It's your stupid coffee."

Megan's green eyes danced. Neither of them was a morning person, but she came to much faster than he did, more than likely because of the espresso. "My coffee's not stupid and it can't act that fast, anyway. Nothing acts that fast except for kryptonite. It's just your natural sunny disposition, taking over."

Coming around to his other side, Megan picked up the remaining notes from Sam's desk. She read them with interest—and with difficulty. With the possible exception of her brother, Rusty, Sam had the world's worst handwriting.

Sam glanced from Cade to Megan. Between them, they'd divided the notes that it had taken him most of the night to pull together.

"Feel free to jump right in." Sam scrubbed his hands over his face, then pushed back from his desk and rose to his feet. It was too late to think about catching a few winks. He'd make it up once the case was over. "I've gotta grab a shower, change my clothes and go see a police detective."

Megan thought of all the times at the Bureau that she'd been forced to work with the local police. It was like rubbing two sheets of coarse sandpaper against each other. Never smooth going.

"They're not exactly high on the buddy system," she reminded Sam.

That was true enough. He remembered his own days on the force. "No, but this one owes me a favor. I dated his sister when no one else would."

He looked at Cade. "You still have that spare shirt and jeans here?"

Cade nodded absently, letting Sam's notes drop back on the desk. He frowned as he looked up at Sam. "Does she realize the odds?"

The question immediately sobered him. The last traces of sleepiness faded.

"I didn't dwell on the ransom thing," Sam admitted. "I figured she's got enough on her mind without bringing that to her attention."

"Bringing what to my attention?"

They all looked toward the doorway. Engrossed in the discussion, they hadn't heard Savannah walk into the outer office. Hadn't seen her enter. Her expression was frozen, like a lost hiker who had just realized that a copperhead was directly in her path.

Cade stepped forward quickly, his hand extended to her. "Ms. King, I'm Cade Townsend." The firmness of his handshake conveyed the mute support he offered. He indicated Megan. "And this is Megan Andreini."

Savannah was scarcely aware of shaking the short blonde's hand. She'd heard something in Sam's voice as she'd walked in just now. Something that chilled her to the bone. She wanted to run from it, to hide, but a perverseness pushed her on. She had to know, know everything. The not knowing was part of this horror she found herself living.

"Bring what to my attention?" she repeated. She looked at Sam pointedly.

"We were discussing another case," Cade told her smoothly.

The lie found no home. The look in Sam's eyes confirmed her suspicions. She'd heard enough when she entered to know they were talking about Aimee.

"No, you weren't," she contradicted. She continued to focus on Sam. "What does it mean when there's no ransom note?"

Cade and Megan exchanged looks. This one was Sam's call. It was his case, and if he wanted her to know, he'd have to be the one to explain it.

Sam put himself in Savannah's place. He'd want to be told.

He chose his words carefully. "It means that whoever took Aimee wanted her, not the money." He watched as awareness dawned and bred horror in her eyes. Sam quickly fell back into textbook jargon.

"Children are kidnapped for several reasons." He enumerated them for her benefit. "To trade in exchange for a ransom, to get even with someone, and to gain custody because a parent has been denied it or wants to deny it to his or her spouse. They're also kidnapped to be sold to a childless couple."

"Sold?" Savannah repeated numbly. What kind of a monster would sell a child? *The same kind who would steal one,* she thought, fighting despair. "But that's slavery," she protested numbly.

"It's buried under a variety of names," Cade told her. "So-called private adoption fees, finders' fees, things like that—but essentially, it's selling. That's not to say that most private adoptions aren't completely aboveboard, but—"

She wasn't listening. "Is that all of them?" Savannah asked, not knowing if she could stand to hear any more. "All the reasons?" she added when Sam didn't respond.

"People also kidnap a child because they've recently lost a child themselves." He thought of one case he'd encountered in which a woman had abducted a newborn after she had gone through all the stages of a fantasy pregnancy and didn't have anything to show for it. "Real or imagined, they want to replace that child with another."

Sam glanced toward Megan, afraid that she'd add the last reason. It was one he didn't want to touch on yet—one that was better left unsaid, especially with Cade in the room. No one needed to be reminded of the kinds of deviates who roamed the earth and preyed on the weak and innocent.

He hoped he would never have to tell Savannah that reason.

Of like mind, Megan held her tongue.

Savannah's head began to ache. The reasons Sam cited, the ones that might apply to her case, drove another large wedge between her and hope. Savannah struggled not to be overwhelmed. She acknowledged the reasons only insofar as recognizing them might be helpful in finding Aimee.

Everything had to have that focus, she thought fiercely.

Savannah's silent anguish was palatable. "Can I offer you a cup of coffee?" Megan asked, moving toward the coffeemaker.

She'd had enough coffee in the last few days to float a battleship. The last thing she needed was more caffeine. Her nerves were brittle enough as it was. Savannah shook her head. "No."

"Wise choice," Sam congratulated her, trying to lighten things a little. "Megan's leftover coffee is used to fill the cracks caused by interstate trucks on the thruways."

Savannah's mouth curved slightly in response. The last several hours, ever since she'd left this office, had knitted themselves into a continuing nightmare. She knew she couldn't go on this way.

She looked at Sam. "You didn't call me." She tried not to sound accusing.

"There was nothing to report yet."

She glanced at the papers that were on his desk. There was an awful lot of writing on them. Absently, she wondered why he didn't use a computer. Funny, the kind of thoughts that went through your head in the middle of a crisis, she thought.

"You haven't made any progress?"

Right about now, faced with the look in her eyes, he would have sold his soul to be in the miracle business. Sam glanced at his watch. "It's only been—"

Savannah held up her hand. She didn't want to deal with excuses. That wasn't why she'd raised the point. "I understand. Not much time has passed since I hired you. But you have to understand that every second is agony for me."

Cade stepped in. "We do understand, Ms. King," he assured her.

Savannah turned toward him. Because she felt he could empathize more closely with her, Cade was the one she'd wanted in the first place. If she couldn't have him, she could at least use Cade's support when she made her request.

"Then tell him to let me come along on the investigation."

Her entreaty, coming out of the blue, caught Cade by surprise. "What?"

Savannah redirected her appeal to Sam. "I came here to tell you that I tried it your way, and I can't do it any longer. I can't sit by the telephone, waiting for that right phone call to come in. I can't go through the motions of living and breathing without being busy doing something." Savannah's eyes swept over

Cade again. He was her best shot. He would understand. He'd gone through it himself. *Was* going through it himself. "The *right* something."

Cade totally empathized with the way Savannah felt, but having her come along would impede the investigation, maybe jeopardize it altogether. He couldn't allow it. "Ms. King—"

He was going to turn her down, she realized. Didn't he remember what it was like, sitting on the side, feeling useless, your insides breaking apart?

She was determined not to be put off. Not again. "You started this agency because you couldn't just stand by and let others handle the case for you. Because you had to feel as if you were doing something productive to try to find your son."

The look in her eyes spoke to Cade more than her words did. She was a person whom inactivity would destroy. He couldn't be responsible for that. And he couldn't truthfully argue with what she'd just said, or even downplay it. He'd been in her place and hadn't been able to endure it, either.

"You've done your homework." There was a note of admiration in his voice.

She didn't want Cade's admiration. She wanted his word. "All I want is equal opportunity to do the same. Please."

Sam made a last-ditch effort. Cade and Megan both knew how he felt about civilians coming along. "You're not an investigator, Ms. King."

The excuse carried no weight. Savannah nodded toward Cade.

"Neither was he when he started." It was Sam who was going to have the final word in this, she realized. Savannah turned her appeal back to him. "I won't get in your way, Sam, I promise. I'll do whatever you tell me to. I just want to be there with you, to know firsthand what's going on, even if it's nothing. I just *have* to be there." Savannah tried to think of a reason he could accept. "Maybe something'll come to me that I've overlooked or forgotten."

It wasn't in her nature to plead, but everything had gone against nature since Aimee had disappeared. She would get down on her knees if she thought it would help sway Sam.

"Please. I can't go home anymore."

"The best thing for you to do," Cade suggested kindly, "is to go back to work and try to keep your mind occupied."

"I do a lot of my work out of the house. I'm a programming engineer and designer, and I can't even remember how to turn on my computer without concentrating. Do you actually think I can get anything done like this?" She didn't wait for an answer. "I've taken a leave of absence until this is over." The time was open-ended, just like her ordeal was.

Sam felt like a man rearranging deck chairs on the Titanic. "Maybe your family—"

"They're tiptoeing around me as if I was going to shatter at any minute. I'm not going to shatter," she said fiercely. "You won't have to treat me with kid gloves if that's what you're worried about. I don't

want to have to deal with sympathy. I want to *do*
something.'' She ran her tongue along her dry lips.

Watching her, a flash of heat licked at Sam, stunning him. The next moment it was gone, and he
thought he had imagined it.

''If it's a matter of money,'' Savannah pressed,
''I'll double your fee.''

''Ms. King—'' Sam began.

''Triple it.'' She'd find the money somehow. She'd
sell the house and mortgage the rest of her life if she
had to.

''It's not the money,'' Sam insisted. ''It might not
be safe—''

''Why should I be any safer than Aimee is?''

Sam had no answer for that.

Listening, Cade was won over. Truthfully, he
couldn't find it in his heart to tell her ''no,'' not after
the very same sentiments had driven him to start this
agency. The case was Sam's, but the agency was his.
And her emotions echoed his own.

In general, Sam knew Cade was not an emotional
man. There were times when Sam didn't have a clue
what the other man was contemplating. This wasn't
one of those times. Looking at him, Sam knew exactly what Cade was thinking. Cade wanted him to
agree to Savannah's request.

Sam resigned himself. Ultimately, Cade called the
shots. Besides, if he were being honest with himself,
it just wasn't in his heart to tell Savannah ''no'' a
second time. It just felt too cruel.

But even as the words formed in his mouth, Sam

had a sinking feeling he was really going to regret this break with tradition.

"All right, you can come with me."

A minor wave of relief swept over her. Savannah released the breath she was holding. Her eyes thanked him even though she didn't say the words out loud. Instead, she turned toward the petite, lively-looking blonde at her side and made another request.

"I'll have that cup of coffee now."

"You got it," Megan told her.

"And I'll grab that shower," Sam said by way of an exit, although by now it was going to take a lot more than just cold water to get him functioning properly again, he thought grudgingly.

Megan measured out a hefty serving of coffee granules and poured them into the coffeemaker. He glanced at the machine as he walked past.

Maybe there was hope after all, Sam mused. One cup of Megan's coffee and Savannah would probably be too numb to want to go anywhere.

Chapter 4

His hair was still damp and curling about his ears and the back of his neck from the shower he'd taken. It'd been more like a quick, three-minute flirtation with pulsating water than a shower, but it was enough to remind him that he could still feel human rather than something the cat had dragged in.

Sam had toweled his body dry and hurried into Cade's clothes. Cade had a couple of inches on him in height and mass, but the fit was close enough.

It was as if there was an inner clock ticking within him, and he didn't want to waste any more time than he absolutely had to. Certainly not on going to his apartment and getting a change of his own clothes.

The inner clock went off every time he took over a new investigation. Hours, minutes, seconds were precious. The more that slipped away, the greater the odds of not finding the child.

That outcome wasn't something he was prepared to accept or even actively entertain. Not because Savannah had looked at him with eyes that were filled with pain, or the fact that she managed to somehow eloquently restrain the fears that he knew had to be ravaging her, but because there was a child out there who'd been wrongfully taken, and with some luck and skill, he could do something to change that.

And he had to give a hundred percent of himself in order to try.

That didn't allow anything to be left over, he thought as he headed out the door with Savannah.

"It's that one over there. The tan one." Leading the way into the parking lot, he pointed out his car for her benefit. His dream was a sports car, a red one. But red cars stood out, and he needed to blend in if he was going to do his job effectively.

The car could stand a wash, he thought as he brought Savannah to it and unlocked the door.

He paused a moment as she slid into the passenger seat, his eyes drawn to her legs. They were shapelier than most. He wondered if she worked out at a gym.

He used to. When there was time. Lately, though, there didn't seem to be enough time to take care of the lesser details in his life, like workouts and car washes. He'd no sooner finish one case than another one walked through the door. Cade had been talking about hiring another investigator, but he hadn't had time to get around to that yet.

Sam was the first to agree that it took a unique individual to do what they did, to immerse themselves in the world of the hopeless and find a path to hope. But the rewards were indescribable. The high that came from seeing a parent reunited with his or her missing child was nonpareil. Though the work was draining and demanded everything from him, he wouldn't have traded his life for anyone's.

But occasionally he needed some time to himself, and wished there were more than twenty-four hours in a day.

Rounding the hood, Sam got in on his side. He sorted through his key ring for the right one, then put it in the ignition and started the car.

Usually, he was too busy to notice the loneliness. And when he wasn't, there was his family—his brothers and sister and their kids and spouses—to plug up the holes in his life. He'd been on the verge of lasting relationships three times in his life, but each time he was always the one to back away first. There was no way he'd ever allow someone he cared about to be subjected to the kind of austere life he led. It was, in essence, the kind of life his father had led. A man who couldn't be there a hundred percent of the time for those he loved shouldn't have a wife, shouldn't have a family. It wouldn't be fair to them.

After garnering three strikes, Sam figured he was out of the game.

But once in a while, when he saw someone like Savannah, he remembered with a touch of fondness just what the game had been all about.

Guilt came less than a beat later, finding him on Culver Drive as he took the main thoroughfare heading south. The woman was literally torn apart because her child was missing, and he was noticing her legs. Sam wasn't exactly sure what kind of a lowlife that made him, but he was fairly certain it was somewhere down there on the food chain.

The silence in the sedan was thick, oppressive. Sam liked silence when it was of his own choosing. This wasn't.

There were things that hovered between them, unsaid, that needed clearing. He waited until he came to the first light, then turned toward her. Her profile, half hidden by her long blond hair, was flawless. And rigid. He felt for her, and told himself he shouldn't. Not if he was going to handle the case properly.

He felt it anyway.

"I just want you to know that just because I've agreed to let you come with me on the investigation, that doesn't mean I've changed my mind about having you along. I'm against this."

She already knew that. Just how was it that he thought she'd interfere? "Why? Can't you use an extra pair of hands?"

Though he was outgoing, he'd never partnered well. It would have been difficult for him to work with even Megan or Cade on a continuing basis. Experience had taught him that he moved more quickly by himself. Having Savannah along was going to change all the rules, all the parameters. He couldn't pretend to be happy about it.

"Not getting tangled up in mine," he told her as he looked back at the road. "This isn't a juggling act, and it doesn't involve manual labor. That's all extra hands are good for."

She'd always been inclined to work with others, although she admittedly did better when she was the one in charge. Being a subordinate was something she wasn't accustomed to. She was willing to do it for Aimee.

"But you could use an assistant, couldn't you?" Savannah pressed.

He switched lanes to get out from behind a truck with the logo of a local supermarket embossed on its side. Sam had made his own assessment of Savannah when she'd first walked into his office. There'd been nothing to change his mind.

"To be honest, you don't strike me as the type of person to take orders very well." He glanced at her and saw the protest rising to her lips. "I know because I'm not either." He supposed that gave them something in common. A half smile curved his mouth. "Kindred spirits know each other, Ms. King."

The formality of being addressed as Ms. King erected walls between them. She didn't want any. She wanted him free to share any thoughts, any theories.

"It's Savannah," she corrected. "And if we're kindred spirits, then you can guess what I'm going through."

The changing light gave him the opportunity to stop and really look at her. His answer was honest. "Not even a clue."

She liked that, liked the fact that Sam didn't presume to put himself in her place by virtue of projection just because that was the easy way. No one who had not been through it could possibly know what it felt like to have a child stolen away from them. Looking back later, she realized that it was this moment when she began opening up her heart to him.

"And I hope you never find out. But making me stay out of this can't be called anything except cruel and unusual punishment, and I think you'd agree that I'm being punished enough."

Her choice of words jumped out at him. "Is that how you see it—as punishment?"

Sam played with the angle. Maybe there was a cult lurking in the background, some sort of religious fanatics that she was, or had once been, associated with. People who sought to "punish" her for some transgression, or for the act of leaving them. There were thousands of angles to explore and thousands of questions he hadn't asked yet. The trick was always being able to find the right ones. It always amazed him the kind of things people left out when they told a story.

"What else could it be?" she retorted, staring at the green digital numbers on his dashboard announcing the time. Almost one-hundred twenty-four hours now. Despite her best efforts, a trickle of irritation broke through. "I wasn't a vigilant mother. If I was going to indulge myself, I shouldn't have brought Aimee along. And if I did bring her along, then she should have been foremost in my every thought, my every movement."

She was being hard on herself. He'd seen it before. It was a common reaction to the situation. "You're only human."

There was no comfort in the excuse for her. "I'm a mother. I'm not supposed to be human." Savannah's lips twisted into a semismile as she recalled something she'd once heard. "I'm supposed to have eyes in the back of my head and wisdom beyond my years."

Sam laughed shortly. "Doesn't sound like any mothers I know. What kind of child-care manuals have you been reading?"

Her mother used to say that—that she needed eyes in the back of her head to keep track of her children. Savannah let out a long, shaky breath as she dragged a hand through her hair.

"Nothing lately. I can't seem to focus long enough to read anything." She looked at him suddenly, needing to hear someone be honest with her. "Do you think we'll find her?"

He kept his eyes on the road. Optimism was something he'd always taken for granted. "I have every hope."

Hope. The biggest four-letter word ever created, she thought cynically. But it was also a smoke screen where the truth was concerned.

"Do you think we'll find her?" she repeated insistently.

The light turned green, but Sam didn't step on the accelerator immediately. Instead, he looked at the woman in the passenger seat. She was asking him for the truth—and praying for a lie if the truth was too difficult to handle.

"Yes." The single word rang within the car like the first church bells at Christmas. The driver in the Range Rover behind him honked his horn. Sam moved his foot off the brake. "I think we'll find her." He would have said it even if he didn't believe it. But he did. "ChildFinders has an excellent reputation." In two years, they'd tracked down twenty-five of the twenty-six missing children they'd searched for. Anyway you sliced it, it was a hell of a record, and he was damn proud of it, damn proud of being associated with the agency.

Savannah sank back into the seat, the rigid features of her face relaxing a little. "Thank you."

"Don't say it yet," he cautioned, then glanced at her in case she misunderstood. "But you will."

The words of caution surprised her. "Are you superstitious?"

He would have been quick to deny that once. There was something unenlightened-sounding about being superstitious. But he was far more at ease with idiosyncrasies than he used to be.

"Only about some things," he admitted. "Never met an investigator or cop who wasn't superstitious in some way about something."

She wanted to know about this man she was putting her faith and trust in. "Have you met many? Policemen, I mean."

He thought of his years on the force and the men he'd worked with, good and bad. "A whole slew of

them. I was a cop, until about a year ago.'' And he
had a newly minted detective's shield when he
walked out.

''What happened?''

He thought of his last case—the one for which he
had almost killed a man with his bare hands. That
man had willingly left a baby to die because it suited
his purposes. But sharing that with Savannah might
make her feel uneasy, so he gave her only half the
truth. It seemed simpler that way.

''The unsolved cases got to me. There's just too
much work to be able to handle anything properly.''
It was the lament of every policeman, every detective.
Some just bore up to it better than others because they
had more patience to spare. Or because they didn't
care. But he did. And that was a problem on its own.
''Even with overtime, I just didn't have the kind of
time I wanted to devote to them. And then Megan
suggested I talk to Cade. The rest, as they say, is
history.''

For a moment, names scrambled in her mind. ''Megan, that's—''

Sam turned right on University Drive. ''The blonde
who tried to poison you with what she calls coffee.''

Savannah nodded. Absently, she wondered if Sam
and the other woman were more than friends. The
next moment she dismissed the thought. It didn't matter. Nothing mattered except getting Aimee back.

The route Sam was taking began to look familiar
to her. She straightened, looking out the window.
''Are we—?''

He thought he detected apprehension in her voice. Maybe he should have tried harder to prevent her from coming along.

"We're going back to the mall."

While still toweling dry, he'd called the Newport Beach police station and been told that Underwood was due in sometime after one. The detective had to be in court this morning to testify in a case. That tabled a meeting between them until later. Sam had reorganized his schedule accordingly.

"Since you insist on coming along, I thought we'd try to re-create every step you took. Maybe something important's gotten lost in the cracks."

It made sense. Savannah braced herself stoically. She hadn't been back to the mall since Aimee disappeared. The very thought of returning drove a chill through her, but Sam was right. Maybe she would remember something by being there that she'd overlooked earlier or forgotten to mention.

That was part of her own bargaining ploy, she realized. That having her along might help her remember. She just hadn't realized how difficult it was going to be, going back.

"When we're finished," Sam was telling her, "if we have nothing new to go on, I'd like a complete list of the names and addresses of your friends and the people you work with—when you do go to the office."

"My friends *are* the people I work with," she told him. "We're pretty much like family." Closer, actually, she thought. She certainly felt closer to some of the people she worked with than she did to her own parents.

"Then that makes it even easier."

Savannah saw no connection between her friends and Aimee's disappearance. They had been nothing but kind and supportive since they'd found out about the kidnapping. "Why?"

He didn't relish explaining this to her. She'd been shaken enough, but it was a very real possibility, and, unless he missed his guess, one she'd have to face eventually.

"Because, according to all the reports I've read and the stories from people in the area where Aimee disappeared, no one saw anything unusual. No one saw a child struggling with an adult."

She knew all about the stories. She'd read and re-read the newspaper articles, and watched every single broadcast that she could. Savannah couldn't begin to understand how no one had seen anything. It was as if her daughter had just vanished into thin air.

"No one even saw Aimee," she said bitterly.

"Exactly. And unless magic has suddenly decided to rear its head in the twenty-first century in an up-scale mall, or everyone's been struck selectively blind, that's not possible." He slowed his speed as morning traffic began to pick up. "Your daughter didn't just vanish. Which means someone had to have seen her—but didn't *know* they were seeing her."

That made even less sense to her. "I'm still not following you."

Sam made a sharp left and brought the car to a stop

in the first parking lot. Weekday mornings the malls were generally empty until almost noon. There were no sales going on the way there usually were in the latter part of the week. Megan had disappeared on a Thursday at the height of the crowd swell—which made her vanishing act even more difficult to believe. For Sam, it all pointed to one thing. *Someone* would have noticed if there'd been a struggling child.

"I think Aimee was taken by someone she knew. Someone you knew."

Savannah looked at him, appalled. "That's not possible. No one I know would do something so horrible." She had no enemies, no friends who were cruel or unbalanced. How could he even suggest something so despicable?

He was vaguely aware of the fact that it pained him to be so blunt with her, to tear away any strands she was clinging to for strength. But it didn't make what he was saying any the less true.

"Everyone's got a darker side, Savannah." He saw the defiant look in her eyes, but a part of her believed him, he thought. "It just takes something to trigger it."

To agree was to shake up her universe. "I won't think that way," she insisted.

He caught her hands in his, dragging her attention back to what he was saying.

"Work with me here. Someone you know follows you to the mall, bides his or her time until your back is turned, then sneaks up and draws Aimee away. He or she tells your daughter that they're going to play a game. A trick on Mommy. She looks like the type who loves games.''

Savannah pressed her lips together. She felt her eyes moistening. ''She is.''

Savannah struggled against what he was saying. She didn't like the way this sounded. It was all too plausible. And too horrible. If she were to believe Sam's theory, then there wasn't anyone left who she could trust, except her parents and sister. Everyone else would be a suspect.

The thought constricted her heart still further.

''All right,'' she agreed, her voice shaky. ''Let's just suppose you're right. That still doesn't explain why no one saw her.''

The answer was simple. ''Because she wasn't Aimee anymore.'' He'd played around with the theory after he'd mentioned it to the hot dog vendor yesterday. ''Maybe the kidnapper put a jacket and a baseball cap on her to hide her hair. Aimee was wearing a pair of jeans and a T-shirt when she disappeared, wasn't she?''

Savannah nodded. ''And a sweatshirt. An Angels sweatshirt.'' At four, her daughter was a devout tomboy who shunned frills.

Savannah fought against the implications of Sam's suggestion. To do something like that required planning. It meant someone had been watching her for a while. Waiting. She couldn't allow herself to believe that.

''Why would anyone do that?''

That was the million-dollar question. ''If we had a

specific reason, then we'd be able to narrow in on who did it.'' The look in her eyes was too painful for his conscience to deal with. He found himself turning away. ''Or at least—'' he sighed, more to himself than to her ''—that's the theory.''

Sam turned to look at Savannah just before he got out of the car. He could guess by the look in her eyes what she was thinking. She was devastated that someone might betray her like this. He would have felt the same way in her place.

''You've got to focus on the positive aspect of that.''

She stared at him as if he'd suddenly lapsed into a foreign language. ''*What* positive aspect?''

''If it's someone you know—someone who's gone to all this trouble and planning to abduct Aimee— they won't hurt her.''

It took her a moment to absorb that, to deal with the thought of betrayal and somehow find hope in it. With one theory, he'd knocked out the foundations of her world and then tried to rebuild on their site.

''Right,'' she said numbly, rallying around the single thought. Aimee was all right. Maybe she was nervous, and missing her mommy, but she wasn't scared. It helped somewhat, believing that. ''But then what are we doing here?''

''It's just a theory,'' he reminded her. ''What we are doing here is eliminating possibilities and checking out part of my theory.'' As Savannah watched, Sam took several sheets of folded paper from his pocket and opened them up for her benefit.

Savannah's mouth dropped open as she looked at the pages, one after the other. "That's Aimee."

Nodding, he took the sheets back. "I'm not much on the computer, but Megan has this program that can morph people, or add and subtract features."

In this case, Sam had disguised the girl in all the possible ways he could come up with at three in the morning. In one shot, he'd eliminated almost all traces of Aimee's long blond hair, and put on a baseball cap—an Angels cap with a flying A. He had a hunch that was what the abductor had used, since Aimee had an affinity for the local baseball team.

"We're going to show these 'photos' around to the vendors and salespeople to see if we can jog a few memories."

He saw a light enter Savannah's eyes for the first time since he'd met her. The pleased feeling that filled him was something he didn't have time to dwell on. He filed it away for later.

"Well, what are you waiting for?" she pressed. "Let's go!"

Sam smiled a little at the eagerness, and hoped it wasn't misplaced. "Yes, ma'am."

Chapter 5

"May I see that one again, please?"

Leaning over a section of the fine jewelry display case, the saleswoman reached for the last altered photograph Sam had shown her.

Savannah didn't bother trying to squelch the bubble of excitement that rose in her chest. She and Sam had been up and down the entire department store, retracing her steps and talking to every salesperson they came in contact with. Especially people whose sections faced one of the three possible exits from the store. But each question they'd asked about that day had been met with a negative response, and Savannah had been close to giving up hope that they'd learn anything here. The sales clerks all looked at the photographs and shook their heads. No one had seen either Aimee, or any of the various altered versions in the photographs Sam had brought.

Until now.

Without realizing it, Savannah urgently laid her hand on the other woman's arm. "Do you recognize her?"

Taking the photograph from Sam, the woman shook her head. "I'm not sure." As she examined it, she held the photograph unusually close.

"Do you wear glasses?" It was more of a guess than a question on Sam's part. His mother used to do that until she'd finally broken down and gotten glasses; it had been a matter of vanity.

The woman flushed as she set the ink-jet photograph on the counter again.

"Contacts, actually," she admitted ruefully. "The smog's been bothering my eyes lately, and I can't keep them in for very long. I start looking as if I've been crying all night."

"Were you wearing contacts on Thursday?" Sam wanted to know.

Savannah's heart sank. She knew where Sam was going with this.

The saleswoman shook her head. "Couldn't. Worse day than today." She glanced down at the photograph again, an apologetic look on her face. "I *think* I saw someone who looked like that leaving Thursday morning. I don't generally notice children, but the reason I noticed was because this one had this giggle—"

The air all but stopped in Savannah's throat. "An

infectious laugh?'' The question tumbled out. ''Did it make you want to laugh, too?''

Sam saw the look on Savannah's face. Elation over their first breakthrough.

''Yes,'' the saleswoman said, looking pleased that she'd been able to help.

Savannah's heart felt as if it was about to burst right out of her chest. She clutched at Sam's arm. ''That's Aimee. Everyone always said she had this wonderful laugh that made people want to laugh along with her. You can't help it when you hear her.''

Bingo, Sam thought. They had their eyewitness.

''Who was she with?'' But the woman began to move her head from side to side. ''Think carefully,'' Sam cautioned her.

''I don't know. I didn't notice the parent—just the child.'' The saleswoman frowned slightly. ''When I looked, I thought it was a little boy.''

''I'm the parent,'' Savannah insisted. ''And I wasn't with her.''

The words broke away from her before she caught herself. She'd promised Sam she wouldn't break down. Savannah struggled to regain control. The woman hadn't meant anything by the remark, and she knew it. It was just that she felt so very frustrated, so very exposed right now.

''Please,'' she begged. ''This is very important. Can't you try to remember?''

Sighing, the saleswoman shook her head. ''I already told you—''

But Savannah wouldn't be put off. She didn't care

what the woman had told her; she'd seen Aimee, and that meant she had to have seen more, too. "A man, a woman—who was holding her hand?"

With a large sigh, the woman closed her eyes, apparently hoping that would somehow help focus her and help her to recall a seemingly insignificant memory, now buried deeply.

But when she opened her eyes again, Sam saw no sudden light of revelation. Only a mute apology. Out of the corner of his eye, he saw Savannah battling dejection.

"I'm sorry," the saleswoman told them sincerely. "I'd only be making it up. I don't remember."

"But the child wasn't struggling?" He wanted to be absolutely sure about that.

"No, I told you, the child was laughing. If I'd noticed that he—that she—" the saleswoman amended "—was struggling, I would have looked at the person with her. Maybe even called security if I thought it was suspicious."

"Thank you." Savannah's disappointment was so strong that Sam felt he could reach out and touch it. Something protective stirred within him. He wanted to take her out of here. "If you remember anything else, you've got my card."

The saleswoman nodded. "From yesterday, right. Shouldn't I tell this to the police?" the woman asked suddenly, as the significance of what she'd just told Sam hit her.

"By all means," Sam agreed. His hand on her elbow, he urged Savannah out of the store.

"It was Aimee, I know it," Savannah insisted. They finally had a piece of information, but it didn't seem to lead anywhere. Savannah was torn between elation and frustration. "Isn't there anything we can do?"

She looked as if she wanted to run in two different directions at the same time. Sam placed his hands on her shoulders to anchor her, forcing her attention back to him. He wanted to focus her on the good part. If she fell apart now, that would cost them time.

"Look, I know you're frustrated, but at least we know that Aimee was all right when she left the store, and that she wasn't afraid. That strongly indicates that she did know the person who took her. That also means that when we find her, there might not be that much of a trauma for her to deal with." He knew that had to be something Savannah was worried about.

When. He had used the word *when.* People had begun to say "if." "If" they found Aimee, not "when." They hadn't said it directly to her, but around her. Savannah had overheard the police detective talking to his partner in the police station when they'd brought her in for questioning on Thursday. Even then, Underwood had said "if" they found Aimee.

The small word had driven a shaft right through her heart.

But Sam didn't believe that the odds were stacked against them, and for that she was eternally grateful to him.

As he saw Savannah raise her eyes to his, Sam felt

something that at any other time he would have described as feeling like an electrical charge. But this wasn't the right setting for one. He was working here, not looking at a desirable woman in the reflection of a smoky barroom mirror.

"Thank you."

The words fairly pulsed in the air between them. "For what?"

He knew "for what," she thought. She said it anyway. "For making it positive."

Sam lifted a shoulder in a dismissive shrug. There was no need to thank him for what he considered standard procedure.

"It's the only way I operate," he assured her.

He glanced over his shoulder. The saleswoman was still looking at them through the glass door. She'd been the last of the people in the store to question. There were no vendors stationed by their carts outside this exit door. It led directly to the parking lot.

Odds were that the kidnapper had hurried Aimee to his car. But nothing was ever written in stone.

Sam nodded toward the cluster of carts gathered inside the outdoor mall. "C'mon, let's show this photograph around to the vendors."

He figured it was a shot in the dark to question them again, but sometimes shots in the dark hit something. Who knew? Maybe they'd get lucky.

They didn't.

An hour of going from one vendor to another with

the photograph that the saleswoman had picked out
had yielded nothing more.

Savannah tried not to give in to the despair rising
within her. She was doing something, and because of
Sam, they had found a new piece of information. That
was all that counted.

She turned toward him as they walked away from
the last vendor. ''Now what?''

It was a toss-up between going to the police station
and going to Big Bytes, the software company for
which she worked. He figured the police station might
be too daunting for her. She needed to see friendly
faces.

''Now we go to see the people you work with.''

To question them, she thought.

But she wasn't about to argue with him on that
score. She was beginning to believe in him. Sam had
been right about the disguise the abductor had put on
Aimee, and it looked as though he was right about
Aimee being kidnapped by someone she knew.

Maybe he was right about where they would find
their kidnapper as well.

She tried to imagine one of the people she worked
with doing this—and couldn't.

How would being questioned about the kidnapping
affect some of her co-workers? She was on friendly
terms with all of them, had gone to their weddings
and their children's birthday parties. They were more
like a family than people who labored side by side
for eight hours a day. She didn't want to offend any
of them.

Savannah got into the car and waited until Sam was behind the wheel.

"How are you going to word this?" She buckled up after he did. "They took up a collection for me to offer a reward for any information leading to the kidnapper's apprehension and conviction."

And Sam just bet the police were thrilled to learn that. An offer like that *really* brought the crazies out. Sam decided to keep that to himself.

Sam guided the car out of the lot. The fact that she was worried about hurting people's feelings told him that she was in control of herself as much as she could be. It was a good sign.

"Don't worry, I'm not about to fling accusations around." He saw that the answer didn't satisfy her. Sam thought a minute. He knew she wouldn't want to tell them he was a private investigator. That would generate the exact impression that she was trying to avoid. "You can introduce me as your friend if you'd rather handle it that way. All I want to do is just get a feeling."

"A feeling?" she echoed, turning in her seat to look at him. "You mean, like a psychic?"

It would be nice if it were that easy, if he could just concentrate and pick up vibrations or whatever it was that psychics claimed to pick up.

"No, more like someone working with hunches." Experience had honed that ability for him. "Mine sometimes pay off." Actually, more often than not— but that would sound like bragging, so he didn't bother mentioning it.

"Like the altered photographs."

He grinned. "Like the altered photographs."

"You're the boss." Containing the urge to fidget, Savannah sat back in her seat. *Just keep me together until this is all over,* she prayed. But she said, "You make a left when you get to MacArthur."

"Savannah, has there been any news?"

Sam stepped back as a tall, moon-faced older man, wearing faded brown slacks that looked as if he'd slept in them more than one night, came up to envelop Savannah in a bearlike embrace. She was all but lost in his arms.

The low, comfortable buzz within the rustically decorated, glass-and-wood office receded as Savannah's presence suddenly became apparent. He heard chairs being scraped back all through the high-ceilinged, two-story room.

It was all Savannah could do not to sink into Larry Abrahms's hug, and sob. She thought of him more as a second father than as her boss. But she wasn't here to cry. She was here because Sam wanted to look around, and because she wanted to prove a point to him. That no one here could possibly be involved in the ugliness that had found her.

Moving her head back, she shook it. "None."

Compassion was etched over his wide face with bold strokes.

"I'm sure the police are doing all they can." And then Abrahms looked at the man next to Savannah—an unspoken question in his deep-set brown eyes.

''This is Sam Walters.'' Savannah didn't like lying,
but the truth was harsher to deal with. So, feeling
awkward, she added, ''A friend of mine.''

''Good.'' Abrahms nodded his head in approval.
''You shouldn't be alone at a time like this.'' The
eyes were kindly, but they still managed to pin Sam
down. If this man had daughters, he pitied any guy
who came to his door, Sam thought. ''I hope you're
doing what you can to comfort Savannah.''

''Absolutely.''

''Sam, this is my boss, Larry Abrahms,'' Savannah
said belatedly.

Abrahms chuckled, and, to Sam's fascination, the
man's rounded belly actually shook.

''More like her mentor.'' The pawlike hand went
around his, completely dwarfing it. ''We like to keep
things informal here.''

It certainly looked that way to him, Sam mused.
The crowd around them was growing, as more and
more people left their desks to gather beside Savannah. Sam watched and listened as people reexpressed
their concern, their support and their offers of help to
her. It appeared that Savannah was well liked by
everyone.

This was good for her, Sam thought, and was making her feel that she wasn't alone. A kidnapping
tended to drive a wall between the victim's family
and the rest of the world, isolating them. It was important not to allow that feeling to become overwhelming.

As for him, he looked at the swelling circle around

Savannah with a discerning eye. On the surface, everyone seemed genuine enough in the concern they expressed. But actors were found everywhere. He reserved final judgment for later.

"What are you doing here?" a dark-haired woman who Savannah had addressed as Angela wanted to know. "Larry said you were taking a leave of absence."

Stumped for a moment, Savannah grasped at the first excuse that occurred to her. "I am, but I remembered that the Kwan project is due next week—"

"Good lord, Savannah, you've got more important things on your mind than a foreign account," Abrahms chided in surprise.

She thought on her feet, Sam observed in appreciation. Not everyone could do that.

"I know, but—"

"No 'but,'" Abrahms cut in. "You're not to give that another thought." He nodded toward the man standing next to him. "Elliott's handling it for you."

Elliott Reynolds, a slight man with thinning brown hair and a subservient manner, had been the second one to come up to Savannah. He appeared even more surprised than Abrahms to see her in the office.

"Elliott's handling all your projects," someone else volunteered. "Won't let any of us touch them."

"It's the least I can do," Elliott told her. His eyes were moist as he looked at her. "Anything you want, Savannah—anything at all, you got. You just have to tell me what you need, you know that."

"I know that," she affirmed. Savannah smiled at

the other man, and Sam caught himself feeling a little envious of Elliott for being on the receiving end of the warmth that he saw pass between them.

Elliott shifted uncomfortably. "Claire feels just awful about what you're going through. Her thoughts are with you. She's been wanting to call you, but she just doesn't know what to say."

Savannah shook her head. "There's no need to explain anything, Elliott. Besides, there really isn't anything anyone can say." Her courage began to flag. It was harder and harder to keep up this facade around people who felt her pain.

She glanced toward Sam, and he nodded ever so slightly. "Maybe you're right," she said to Abrahms. "Maybe I'd better go home. There might be some word...." Her voice trailed off before it broke.

Moved, Elliott took her hand in his and squeezed it. "She's all right, Savannah. I just know it." Several others echoed his sentiments.

Savannah took a deep breath. With all her heart, she wished she could believe that. "I hope you're right, Elliott."

Elliott appeared absolutely convinced of what he was saying. "I am. Trust me." His eyes held hers. "Still no ransom note?" Savannah merely shook her head. Elliott looked as if he was searching for something positive to say. "Maybe whoever took her is lonely, and just wants someone to take care of."

"He has a point," Sam told her.

"Of course I do." Something akin to a smile passed over the pale face as Elliott glanced in Sam's direction. But his attention was refocused on Savannah. "You've got to hang on to that, Savannah. That Aimee's alive and well and that everything's going to be all right."

She took a deep breath to steady the nerves that were unraveling again. "I will."

Because the moment called for it and it seemed so natural, Sam slipped his arm around her shoulders. If she was surprised, she didn't show it. Instead, she accepted the mute support and allowed him to usher her out. He'd done it purely to perpetuate the illusion that he was trying to create, but the contact between them seeped into his consciousness.

The heat that flared through him, shooting through his limbs, came as a complete surprise.

Dropping his arm to his side the moment they were out the door, Sam walked briskly in front of Savannah to his car. He didn't like surprises. Any surprises. Even pleasant ones. To be surprised meant to be unprepared, and he always liked being prepared.

The car was unlocked, but he opened the door for her anyway. She was the kind of woman men still opened doors for, despite her independent air—or maybe in diffidence to it. He looked down at her as she slid in.

"Elliott sounds as if he's got a crush on you."

"Elliott?" Where had he gotten that idea? She couldn't envision Elliott having a romantic notion in his head. Savannah laughed softly to herself, as Sam got in on the other side. "Hardly. Elliott Reynolds is my closest friend at Big Bytes."

A Hero for All Seasons

"Oh?" At first glance, they didn't seem to have anything in common. She was a classy lady, and Reynolds was a bland, nondescript little man who probably got overlooked a great deal. Men like that tended to fade into the woodwork around anyone with the least bit of color to them.

"Yes, he took me under his wing when I came to work for the company. He's really very brilliant, you know. He can work magic with a computer."

That Sam could readily believe. But it didn't exclude the other possibility. "Doesn't mean he can't have feelings."

Sam was wrong, dead wrong. What bothered her was that if he could be wrong about this, then he could be wrong about other things. About Aimee. She tried not to think about that.

It was easier trying not to breathe.

"If he does," she told him tersely, "the feelings are directed toward his wife, Claire. Elliott's completely devoted to her." Almost too much so, she thought. "To their daughter, too."

Sam felt a trace of disappointment. "He has a daughter?"

She nodded. Savannah stared out the window. Was it her, or did everything look a little grayer?

"Emily's a little older than Aimee. They would play together every time we got together socially." Her voice hitched as she remembered watching Aimee and Emily at the company picnic last fall. Aimee followed Emily around with the dogged faithfulness of a little sister.

"And they'll play together again," Sam promised her.

Savannah raised her head, determination in her eyes. She had to stop this, had to stop dwelling on the dark side. Sam was right, Elliott was right. Aimee would be back in her arms again. Soon.

"Yes, they will."

That was better, he thought. Her voice sounded stronger. "So tell me more about the people you work with. How long have you known them?"

She didn't even have to pause to think. "Six years. I was the last one hired. Straight out of college." Was that nervous girl back then really her? It was hard to believe. Abrahms had conducted the interview so informally that she'd found herself at ease almost instantly. "The group has stayed pretty much together. Larry likes to think of it as one happy family."

"And is it?"

He was looking for dirt, but there wasn't any. There couldn't be. "Yes, it is. Since I've been here, I've attended five weddings and three baby showers—not counting my own." They'd gone all out for her, making no issue of the fact that she was a single mother. "And two funerals."

His ears perked up. "Funerals?"

"Deaths in the family. Parents," she clarified. "I know these people very, very well. None of them would do this to me."

For her sake, he wanted that to be true, but then that would leave them at square one again.

Sam slowed the car as they came to a stop behind

a line of cars funneling into one lane because of construction on this side of the road. It was too late to take an alternative route.

He turned toward her. "Did you meet Aimee's father at work?"

She shifted in her seat, uncomfortable. "No, I met Aimee's father in college. I was working on my master's," she added.

He could tell by her tone that she didn't want to talk about it, but he wanted his gaps filled in. All of them. "He was a grad student?"

"A professor. I was doing an independent study program, and he was independently studying me." She looked at him in exasperation. She didn't feel like being probed. They'd already established that this didn't have anything to do with Aimee's disappearance. "Is this really necessary?"

"I'm just trying to get a fuller background, but no, strictly speaking, it's not necessary." Not to the investigation at any rate. But if he were being honest with himself, he was having more questions about the woman beside him than the circumstances of the case generated.

But that, he thought, was his problem—not hers. He was going to have to watch that.

Chapter 6

Sam would rather not have taken Savannah with him when he went to see Ben Underwood at the police station, but there didn't seem to be any way around it if he wanted to meet with the detective today.

Tall and on the lean side—though Sam thought of them as pretty evenly matched—Detective Ben Underwood of the Newport Beach Police Department had a boyish look that by all rights he should have long outgrown. The quick grin and unlined face seemed somehow misplaced on a police detective. It tended to make people think of Ben as more of a tall Boy Scout than an officer of the law.

But Ben was sharp. Sam knew that firsthand. Ben also didn't readily welcome outside interference, and, like it or not, Sam knew he was now considered an outsider. Ben would immediately know Savannah had hired him to help on the case.

"What brings you here, Sam? Getting nostalgic for the smell of police blotters?" Ben drawled as he gave Sam a long once-over. Pushing his chair back, Ben rose to his feet before Sam answered.

Sam nodded a greeting. They'd been friends once, but that was a long time ago. They'd gone their separate ways once out of the academy, crossing paths only occasionally.

Sam kept it simple and played along because he knew the rules of the game. You didn't move out of turn unless it was absolutely necessary. "Ms. King hired me to help look for her daughter."

Ben's blue eyes shifted to Savannah. She looked more tired, but he noticed that there was something in her eyes now: a determination that pushed aside the panic and hopelessness he'd seen previously. He wondered if there was a reason for that.

Was Sam on to something?

"Wasting your money, ma'am," Ben told Savannah politely. "Sam's good, but he's not about to find anything that we don't." Deep, piercing blue eyes looked into hers, delving. "We're doing all we can to find your daughter." To back the statement up with physical evidence, he nodded at the tall stack of perforated papers on his desk. Given the nature of her work, he figured she'd recognize computer printout when she saw it. "Those are the phone company records of all the people who've called your toll-free number and your house since your daughter's kidnapping.''

Kidnapping.

Savannah tried not to shiver at the sound of the harsh word. Maybe it was absurd, but she'd been using euphemisms, even in the privacy of her own mind. ''Kidnapping'' sounded so hopeless. So final.

''I've got people looking into their backgrounds,'' Ben was saying. His message was clear. Though overworked, the police department still had far more manpower at their disposal than Sam did.

Savannah bit her lip. Hope was taking a roller coaster ride right over her heart. ''And did you find anything?''

There were a few people in the stack who had piqued his interest, but it was far too early in the game to tell if that amounted to anything. It was against Ben's nature to carelessly raise hopes without backup.

''We're looking into it,'' Ben replied guardedly.

Their eyes locked then, but she knew he wouldn't tell her. Savannah raised her chin.

''Which is why I hired Sam and his agency. They might not find anything faster, but at least he'll tell me what it is when he does come across it.''

Sam avoided her eyes. That wasn't strictly true. Like Ben, Sam felt that some things had to be worked out first before they were conveyed. Very gently, he moved Savannah out of the way, and took out the altered photograph that the saleswoman had recognized. As Ben watched him in silence, Sam unfolded the sheet and offered it to him.

Underwood raised his eyes to Sam in question.

"You might tell your men that Aimee King probably looked more like this when she was taken from the area," Sam told him.

Underwood took the photograph and examined it more closely, then looked at Savannah. His brows drew together in a dark, puzzled line. The child in the photograph had on a baseball cap and a jacket with an Angels logo. "I thought you said she just had on a hooded sweatshirt and jeans—"

"She did," Sam cut in. He didn't want Underwood badgering Savannah, so he proceeded to tell him about how the saleswoman had recognized the doctored image.

Underwood bit back a curse. The kidnapper had disguised the little girl. The angle was so simple that he'd overlooked it completely. The accusation was ripe in his voice when he asked Sam, "How long have you known?"

"For about an hour or so. I came to you first thing," Sam volunteered angelically.

Maybe he did at that. Ben had never known Sam to lie—although that didn't mean that Sam didn't. "Mind if I hang on to this?"

Sam smiled magnanimously. "I insist on it." Sam took Savannah's elbow. "And if you hear anything—"

Underwood looked at him sharply. Sam knew procedures better than he did. "I can't tell you anything, you know that, Sam."

Looking over his shoulder, Sam inclined his head.

"I know. I also know you probably still have my home number. It's been a long time since we talked. As friends," he added pointedly. "Friends who go back a long way. I'll see you around."

"Hold it!" Ben called after him. He was going to want to question the saleswoman. "What did you say the saleswoman's name was?"

"I didn't." Satisfied that he'd driven his point home, Sam added, "It's Gladys Pease."

As Sam ushered Savannah out the tinted glass door that led into the squad room, Ben was writing down the woman's name on his blotter.

Savannah pulled her arm free and looked at Sam. "That's it?" she demanded. "You just give him the photograph and you leave?"

Rather than stand and argue with her, Sam led the way out of the two-story building. He figured she would have to follow.

She did, although when he looked over his shoulder, she didn't appear very happy about it.

"I have the photographs saved on the hard-drive." He knew that wasn't why she was annoyed. She thought he had retreated. But it wasn't a matter of retreating; it was a matter of knowing who you were dealing with. Getting to his car, Sam turned around. "Besides, Underwood doesn't know anything new."

She didn't see it that way. Sam should have pressed him. "He said he was checking out things."

He got in and waited until she followed suit. It took a minute. He figured she was working off her head of steam.

"If there'd been anything," Sam continued once she was inside, "he would have looked more confident. Underwood and I go back a ways. When he's on to something, there's this look in his eyes—like he's on a treasure hunt and he's holding on to what he thinks is the right key." Lucky for Ben that he didn't play poker, Sam mused as he started the car. "That look wasn't there."

"A look?" she echoed. "You're basing all this on a look?"

"No, I'm basing this on a look that *wasn't* there," Sam corrected. "You're paying me for experience, remember?"

Disappointment poured through her like hot, sticky glue, threatening to paralyze everything inside her. "Then he was lying?"

Sam didn't quite see it as lying. "He was being diplomatic. As diplomatic as Ben's capable of being." Diplomacy wasn't Underwood's strong suit. Solving crimes was. "And, like as not, there are probably more than a few people he wants to check out. One thing's certain—"

She was trying very hard to rally, but she was beginning to feel terribly worn around the edges. "What's that?"

"Underwood does have more manpower to check out the people on the lists than we do." He thought of the program Megan had enhanced for their purposes. The one she'd managed to "borrow" from sources that were best left unmentioned. "Still, it wouldn't hurt to get a printout ourselves, and run the names through the program for convicted felons.'' There were favors he could call in for that. And a few more he could trade.

"Convicted felons?'' Savannah's stomach tightened.

He heard the strained note in her voice. "I prefer going with the theory that she knew her abductor, but the bottom line is that we don't know who we're dealing with yet. This kidnapping could have been personal, or it could have just been random. Something about Aimee caught their eye.''

"But the clothes—'' If they had children's clothes with them, didn't that mean that the abduction was planned?

Sam played devil's advocate. In order to be effective, he had to. No theory was ever airtight. "Lenard's has a children's section, doesn't it? The clothes could have come from there.''

Shoplifting was done all the time, despite safe guards, Sam thought. It wouldn't have taken much for the kidnapper to have grabbed the clothes, taken Aimee into the bathroom, and made the change.

"Then it was all spur-of-the-moment?'' Defeat echoed in Savannah's every word. That meant that they hadn't really made any headway at all.

"Could be, although the theory is a little out there.'' Still, Savannah had to be made aware of all the possibilities.

The numbness she felt gave way to an emotional wave. "What are you doing to me? You yank me up, then you push me down—''

He pulled over to the side of the road and unhooked his seat belt. Because he saw the tears in her eyes, he tried to take her into his arms the way he would anyone who was hurting. She fought him off, vainly pounding her fists against his chest before finally sinking against him. She didn't sob, but the breath she pulled into her lungs was shaky.

He waited until her breathing became a little steadier. "I said it wasn't going to be easy."

"I'm sorry," she whispered, afraid that if she spoke any more loudly, her voice would break. "I won't do that again. I want to know, I really do. It's just that..."

She didn't need to explain. He understood. "I know." Very gently, using the tip of his thumb, he wiped away the single tear that had trickled down her cheek. "My fault. I shouldn't be firing all these different things at you at once."

"No, it's all right, really. Keep firing," she urged. Her mouth curved slightly. "I'll be thicker-skinned, I promise."

He couldn't resist tracing the path her tear had taken just once more. "Your skin's fine just the way it is," he assured her softly.

Then, as if voicing the sentiment made him uncomfortable, Sam abruptly released her and started the car up again.

For just a moment there, he'd wanted to kiss her. To hold her and tell her that everything was going to be all right. He had no right to make promises like that, Sam thought, annoyed.

I already have, he reminded himself.

Clearing his throat as he got back into the flow of traffic, Sam kept his eyes on the road.

"There is a possibility that the kidnapper put in a call." She was sitting perfectly still. Sam could feel her eyes on him, waiting for him to continue. "Whoever took Aimee might be having second thoughts after seeing you on television, and just doesn't know how to go about undoing what's been done."

How could they not know? Savannah shifted in her seat to face him. "Why can't they just let her go? Put her out on the street somewhere?"

But as soon as she said it, the thought chilled her. She didn't want Aimee wandering around aimlessly on the streets. There were so many dangerous neighborhoods, places where Aimee could disappear without a trace. Savannah had always believed in the best in people, had always *wanted* to believe in the best. But she was being sorely tested. And right now, she felt as if she was failing.

"They could," he allowed, "but if they took her because they felt something for her—because they wanted a child of their own and then felt guilty about it—then they wouldn't want to endanger her safety like that." Sam readjusted his rearview mirror. The setting sun was behind them and gleaming against the glass. He looked at her pointedly. "There are still a great many possibilities to look into."

She needed more than nebulous assurances. She needed examples. Savannah instinctively trusted him to be honest with her. "Like?"

He thought a second as he slowed the car to a stop at the light.

"Like one of those people who called might know something, and is trying to tell you without implicating someone else." People didn't want to condone the crimes of someone they loved, but turning them in was extremely difficult. It was a catch-22 situation. "That's one of the things the police are looking into."

He smiled at her, remembering. "By the way, I didn't thank you for that vote of confidence you displayed back there—when you told Underwood why you came to the agency," he elaborated in case she wasn't following him.

She didn't see it as a reason for thanks. "Well, it's true. If I hadn't felt as if they were sweeping me to the side, I might not have come to you." Savannah thought about what she'd said for a moment, then changed her mind. "No, that's not true. I would have. I read about the agency a couple of months ago." And had been very impressed by the story—and their record. "Aimee and I took a three-day holiday, renting a house at the beach. I brought along all the old, back issues of magazines I hadn't had a chance to look through."

Something else they had in common, he thought. He'd had a stack himself—until he'd thrown it all out one day after admitting that by the time he had the opportunity to go through them all, the articles would be hopelessly outdated.

"How many did you get to?"

The smile on his lips told her he already knew the answer.

"One, but it was the right one. There was an article on ChildFinders in it." She thought for a second. "It must have been a fairly old article, because it said Cade only had one assistant."

He squinted, trying to read the name of the street as he passed it. *Alder.* Good, he was heading in the right direction.

"I came into the agency a year ago." The anniversary date was almost here, he thought. It amazed him how quickly the time had gone by. "This vacation," he asked with interest, "you took it alone?"

She found the inclination to bristle at his personal questions lessening. She was getting accustomed to probing, she decided stoically.

"As a matter of fact, we did. Elliott and his family were supposed to come, but at the last minute, he canceled. Something about Claire not feeling well. Aimee was really disappointed that she wouldn't have Emily to play with." She'd tried very hard to make it up to her daughter. It was one of the reasons nothing got read, except for the important article. "I think Elliott's a little henpecked, actually," she confided. It made her feel sorry for Elliott. He was a good man who deserved a woman who appreciated him, not ordered him around. "From what I've seen of her and what Elliott says, his wife is rather domineering."

"Not shy and retiring like you?" Sam bit back the soft laugh that accompanied his comment. He'd broken another one of his rules and gotten too friendly.

He was going to really have to watch himself around her. "Sorry, didn't mean that. You're not domineering."

"No, I'm not." Savannah felt herself growing defensive. She tried to bank down the instinct. It wasn't easy. "I am, however, independent. You would be, too, if you were a single parent with a daughter to raise. A daughter who looked to you for everything." She was silent for a minute, then relented. Maybe she was being too hard on him. "You're not the first one who's said that. George thought so, too."

"George?" He repeated the name with interest. She hadn't mentioned a George before. "Does this George have a last name?"

With all that had happened, she'd completely forgotten about George. George Cartwright had been the complete antithesis of Aimee's father: solid, where Jarred had been dark and dangerous. Savannah saw it as a flaw in her character that she'd found dark and dangerous more compelling.

"Cartwright," she replied. "But George has been out of the picture for several months now. He was just someone I went with for a while." Actually, it had gotten more serious than that. She had gone out with George for almost a year before he'd proposed. Savannah had accepted, until she'd realized that it just wouldn't work. "I thought he might make a good father for Aimee."

"What about a good husband for you?"

She had no idea who would make a good husband.

Savannah only knew who wouldn't. "I told you, Ai-mee comes first."

He let that go for now. Traffic became sparser as he drove up a winding path. "So, what happened?"

She backed out, that was what happened. Marrying George would have been wrong and unfair to both of them. Especially to George. He was a good, kind man who deserved better. In her own way, she supposed she loved him. She was just not *in* love with him— and that made the difference.

Savannah shrugged, unwilling to let Sam that far into her life.

"I thought I could settle for a situation like that. I couldn't. I suppose it was petty of me. He would have made a really good father."

"You wanted romance." Most people did; Sam saw no shame in that. "I don't see that as petty. That's pretty normal from where I'm sitting."

Savannah pressed her lips together. Things might have been so different if she'd said yes. "Maybe if I'd married him..."

He caught the doubt in her voice. "What? Aimee wouldn't have been kidnapped?" She couldn't keep beating herself up this way. "And if I were six inches tall and blue, I could have been a Smurf. You can't think that way."

She stared at him. "A what?"

Just the sound of the name made her laugh. A little of the tension slipped away from her and she was grateful to him for that. For making her laugh for no reason at all, when she felt herself being crushed by the weight of her situation.

"A Smurf." Glancing at her, he saw that there was no sign of recognition. It astounded him. "One of those little blue people who ran around in white caps, oversize shoes and pants, no shirts." Still nothing. "Don't tell me you never watched Saturday morning cartoons as a kid." She was a little younger than he was. That meant she should have been familiar with the same shows he'd grown up with.

Savannah shook her head. It had been the source of more than one battle at her house when she was a child, but one she'd always been doomed to lose. Especially since her sister had sided with their parents.

"My parents were into public television programs only. It was a pretty straitlaced childhood." And one in which affection was something that was assumed, not demonstrated. She'd grown up without cartoons—and without hugs.

It sounded deadly dull. "You don't know what you missed. Every single Saturday morning, there I was, in my pajamas, glued to the set, clutching a box of cereal and watching talking stuffed animals solve crimes, and a moose and squirrel outsmarting a couple of very pale-looking, inept spies."

She could visualize him doing that, a cute, tow-headed little boy, being amused by impossible characters and improbable scenarios. If she tried, she could almost hear him laughing. A warmth filtered through her.

Watching cartoons. It sounded so good, so normal.

She'd watched them herself with Aimee, determined to give her daughter the kind of rounded childhood she'd never known. Cartoons and hugs and kisses were always on the agenda.

Savannah smiled at him. "Sounds like a perfect childhood."

"It was," he agreed. "Till my dad died."

He'd said it so matter-of-factly, it took her a moment to realize the import of the words. "I'm sorry."

Yeah, so was Sam. He'd been eleven at the time. Thirteen, before he'd stop blaming his father for dying. "He was a cop, too. Died in the line of duty."

She looked at him. Questions began to rise in her mind. Questions about this man who was swiftly becoming such a central force in her life. "Why did you become a policeman?"

"Seemed a good way to honor his memory. Made me feel closer to him, I guess." He shrugged. "I stopped being one when it didn't work for me any more. I couldn't live by all the straight and narrow rules he did." A distant smile played on his lips. It seemed to work its way right through to her core. She could feel his smile. "He was the straightest man I ever knew."

Stopping the car, Sam pulled up the hand brake to punctuate his statement.

She'd been too engrossed in the conversation and her own feelings to notice the route he'd been driving. Her mouth dropped open as she looked out of the car. "You brought me home?"

"You look tired, and I haven't had a chance to eat

a full meal yet.'' At last inventory, there was only a half-empty box of doughnuts waiting for him at home. That meant he'd have to get some takeout on the way, if he wanted to eat. "I thought we might call it a day for now."

Savannah got out of the car slowly. She didn't relish going inside. Without Aimee, the house was much too quiet for her to bear. She'd turned down the offer to stay with her parents, or to have one of them stay with her. She was grateful to her father for all that he had done. But outside of her endeavor to be part of her father's life, which ceased at a young age, she'd never really been close to either one of them. Having one of them here would mean that she would have to continue putting on a brave front. She just wasn't up to that right now.

But suddenly, she didn't want to be alone. She didn't want to be forced to face the shadows again, the way she had the other nights. She wanted a few more minutes' reprieve.

She wanted, she realized, for Sam to stay with her, at least for a little while. Having him near kept the shadows away.

Savannah looked at him. "The least I can do is fix you something to eat."

"You don't have to bother."

"No bother." The denial tumbled out a little too quickly. "I need something to do," she said honestly. "And I'm not too bad in the kitchen."

Sam had a feeling that the lady was probably good in every room in the house.

The thought had snuck up on him, telling him he was more tired than he thought. He'd taught himself how to do with little to no sleep, but eventually it had a way of catching up on him. He figured he'd just reached "eventually."

The best thing he could do, Sam knew, was drop her off and go home to sack out. But the look in her eyes asked him to stay, to talk to her and keep the bad thoughts at bay. He found that he couldn't say "no" to her. She'd become animated in the car toward the end; there'd been life in her face, and he had a feeling that she was downright beautiful when she laughed.

He knew that had nothing whatsoever to do with the case, but he wanted to see her laugh just once before they permanently parted company.

For now, he'd settle for a sandwich. "All right, if you really don't mind. Nothing fancy." Rounding the trunk, Sam followed her to the front door. "I'm pretty easy to please."

"That would have been my guess." Savannah took out her key.

Just as she began to insert it in the lock, she could hear her phone ringing through the door.

Chapter 7

The key ring slipped from Savannah's fingers, and she nearly dropped it. Sam started to catch it, but she blocked him with her shoulder. Irritation flashed through her.

"I can open my own damn door," she bit off, annoyed with her own clumsy reaction. She couldn't keep falling to pieces like this.

Adrenaline pumped through her tired body as she raced to the telephone in the living room, leaving Sam on her doorstep to find his own way in.

Grasping the receiver, she yanked it from the cradle. "Hello?"

In response, she heard a high-pitched whine, like a radio frequency that was too high to properly be channeled to its receiver. "She's all right," said a metallic voice. A quick click resounded in her ear, aborting all hope for an instant trace.

Savannah clutched the receiver with both hands. "Hello? Hello? Who are you? Please, let me talk to Aimee," she begged even though she knew it was futile. "Let me talk to my daughter!"

A dial tone buzzed in her ear.

Realizing who had to be on the other end of the line, Sam had jumped over the coffee table to reach Savannah's side. But the line was already dead when he took the receiver from her. Frustration bit down hard. He replaced the receiver just as the recording came on to advise him that if he wanted to make a call, he needed to hang up and dial again.

"It was the kidnapper." Stunned, Savannah turned to look at him. The kidnapper had called to tell her that Aimee was all right. Why was he torturing her like this? Why couldn't he just let her daughter go?

"What did he say?" Sam took hold of her by the shoulders in case she was going to faint. "How do you know it was the kidnapper?"

Savannah blinked, feeling like one in a trance. "Because he said she was all right."

"And?" Sam pressed.

"That's all. Just that Aimee was all right."

"Those were his exact words?"

She nodded. "He said, 'She's all right.' Nothing else."

He heard her voice cracking. "Savannah, it might—"

She raised her eyes to his. Savannah knew what he was thinking.

"Be a prank call? No, I don't think so. Whoever called was using one of those synthesizers to disguise their voice. It sounded like a robot, only worse. There'd be no reason to disguise his voice if it was just a prank." And then it hit her. "If he's using a synthesizer, then he's afraid I might recognize his voice."

"Maybe," Sam agreed. It was a distinct possibility. "And it could also be to disguise the fact that it's a woman. Those synthesizers make everyone's voice sound the same."

Someone she knew. A man or a woman. She knew a lot of people. Had her share of neighbors. The field was narrowing, but it still loomed large.

She felt like hitting something. "Why would he call?" she demanded, whirling on Sam. "Why is he doing this?" She wet her lips, suddenly hopeful. "Do you think he is feeling guilty?"

Sam was already dialing the police station. "There's a good chance." And then he stopped, halfway through. He looked at the small LCD screen mounted above the keypad. "You have Caller I.D."

"Yes!" she cried. In the confusion, she'd forgotten all about that.

"I doubt that the kidnapper is calling from home. It's probably a phone booth, but it wouldn't hurt to investigate." Hitting the review button, he watched as a number materialized. Savannah was looking over his shoulder. He pointed to the number. "Mean anything to you?"

She shook her head.

"Maybe it'll mean something to the police." Pressing the numbers for the police station again, Sam glanced at his watch to pin down the time.

"Detective Ben Underwood, please." The operator who answered put him on hold. Sam covered the mouthpiece and turned toward Savannah. "The police are recording all your incoming calls, Savannah. They might be able to detect something in the speech pattern."

She held out little hope. "I heard a screeching noise in the background."

It wasn't his field of expertise, but he had a healthy respect for the capabilities of the people in the police labs. With enough time and equipment, they might be able to filter out the distortions. "Never underestimate the power of technology. It's a wonderful thing."

Savannah could only nod. Suddenly wide-awake and not knowing what to do with herself, she looked toward the kitchen. And then she remembered. "I promised you something to eat."

With his free hand, he waved away her words. Savannah looked drained. "Forget it. I can grab something to eat on the way home."

"No. No," she repeated firmly. "A promise is a promise. You have to eat."

And she had to do something with her hands before she permanently knotted her fingers together, she thought, walking away.

Savannah opened the refrigerator door and stared inside at the near-empty shelves. She had to concentrate to keep from zoning out like a woman in a dream. In a nightmare, she amended.

C'mon, Savannah, pull yourself together. This isn't like you. You can do better than this. Function, damn it. Function!

Pushing aside the horror that threatened to engulf her, Savannah reached for an apron hanging from a magnet hook on the side of the refrigerator. She focused on what she could use to make a meal. Everything in her refrigerator was more than four days old and beginning to either wilt, prune or turn.

She was going to have to go to the supermarket. The task seemed so mundane and yet so out of reach.

Get with it.

She needed to keep up her own strength, she lectured herself silently. What good would she do Aimee if she came apart? Aimee needed a functioning mother when they found her.

When.

Savannah looked up when she heard Sam walk in.

He read the question in her eyes. "Underwood's on it." He'd caught Ben just as the detective was about to go home. "He's going to take the tape to a specialist." That was two jumps he'd gotten on Ben. There had to be a favor in there somewhere—something he could trade on in the future, Sam mused.

Giving up her search, Savannah took out a carton of eggs from the refrigerator and placed it on the counter. Half-empty, it was followed by an onion and

one green pepper, still fairly firm. A small bit of ched-
dar cheese completed the ensemble.

"I can make you an omelette," she offered. She
nodded toward the refrigerator. "I don't have much
else to work with."

He'd always had a weakness for omelettes, and the
more things in it, the better. "Anything's fine. I'm
hungry enough to eat belt buckles."

Cooking had not come easily or naturally to her.
She was better at the computer than at the stove. She
supposed that made her a modern woman.

"I'll try not to make it taste that way," she murmured. Taking out a chopping board, she began dic-
ing the green pepper.

Other than when he stopped in an occasional restaurant, Sam wasn't accustomed to having someone
wait on him. "Need help?"

"No, I can manage." And chopping the green pepper felt oddly therapeutic. But his offer echoed in her
head, registering. She stopped chopping. "You
cook?"

That was stretching the description. He boiled.
Usually those handy little bags that promised meals
in five minutes. And he dialed—takeout.

Sam shrugged evasively. "Enough to survive."

Since she didn't want his help, Sam sat down at
the bar running along the other side of Savannah's
work counter. He looked around, taking in the surroundings for the first time. The kitchen was twice as
large as the one in his eldest brother's house, and
there were five people in David's family. This was

way too much house for just one woman and one little girl.

A quick survey told him that she had money, something he already knew. Since no ransom calls had come in, it confirmed the theory he'd already advanced. That Aimee's abduction had been committed to get the child, not for any monetary rewards.

The playing field was still wide enough to house three football stadiums.

"How do you stay so optimistic?"

Savannah's question dispersed his thoughts for the time being.

He didn't have to think before answering. "It's the only way I know how to operate. Being negative paralyzes you."

That was true enough. Breaking four eggs in the pan, she watched them sizzle hypnotically.

"I know," she murmured quietly. Taking a spatula, she quickly broke up the yolks, moving mechanically. Grateful to have something to occupy her. The diced pepper, cheese and onion were swiftly folded in and partially obscured.

The extension on the kitchen wall jangled. Savannah caught her breath as she jerked her head up. Was it the kidnapper again?

Sam was off the stool immediately.

"I'll get that," he told her. But when he picked up the receiver, there was no one there. "Probably a wrong number."

The frustration he felt was echoed in her eyes. He replaced the receiver. Her number, he knew, was unlisted. That didn't seem to stop anyone. If experience was any yardstick, the calls could well continue into the small hours of the night.

He looked at her. "You're not going to get any sleep unless you turn off the telephone."

How could he even suggest that? "I can't turn off the phone. What if the kidnapper calls back? What if he wants to talk this time?"

That was doubtful, but Sam kept that to himself.

Judging where the dishes would be kept, Sam opened up an overhead cabinet. He guessed wrong and tried the next one with more success.

As he took down two plates, he made a decision.

"I could stay the night. Spend it on your couch in the living room and pick up the calls," he added quickly in case she thought he was suggesting something else. The last thing she needed to worry about was having to fend off unwanted attention.

Savannah looked at him. "Don't you have to check with your wife? Or is she used to this sort of thing?"

"Neither. I don't have a wife *because* of this 'sort of thing.' I couldn't ask a woman to put up with this kind of a life."

The way he said it made her think that there once had been a woman he'd wanted to ask to share this kind of a life, but hadn't. Apparently things hadn't turned out for him, either. It made her feel closer to him somehow.

"If she loved you enough, it wouldn't be too much to ask."

His eyes met hers. "I never got far enough into a relationship for that to be a question."

She knew by his tone that he was telling her the subject was closed. Savannah respected his privacy and backed away.

The idea of having him here through the night was far more comforting than she would have expected. But she still had to turn down his offer. "I can't ask you to do that."

"You're not asking," Sam pointed out. "I'm offering. Part of the service," he added before she could say no again.

He'd looked tired when she'd come into his office this morning, and they had since put in a full day together. "But you need to sleep, don't you?"

That was the least of his problem. If he examined it, the problem went far deeper, was far more intricate than just his catching a few *zzz*s.

So he didn't examine it; he just went with gut instincts. The lady deserved a night's rest.

"I can sleep hanging off a meat hook if I have to. I figure your couch is more comfortable than that." He placed the dishes on the counter for her. He saw the look in her eyes. She was only partially here. "We'll find her, Savannah."

Savannah tried to keep her mind on distributing the omelette evenly. It was an effort doomed to failure. "You keep saying that." She slid the empty frying pan into the sink. Ordinarily, she'd wash it immediately, but that required more strength than she had at her disposal right now.

"That's because I keep believing it." He smiled into her eyes. "And you need to hear it." Taking a bite, he found that the omelette was delicious.

"Yes, I do." She tried to take a couple of bites, but the food wouldn't go past the lump in her throat. Giving up, Savannah placed the fork down on the plate. "Oh, damn, you made me want to cry."

He stopped eating and turned his stool to face her. "Then cry."

She raised her chin, determination etched into her features. "I can't. I won't."

"Why? Because it's weak? It's not weak, Savannah," he told her softly. "It's getting rid of tension. People do all sorts of things to get rid of tension. They go to shrinks, they pop pills, some overeat," he enumerated. He gave up fighting the desire to hold her. Sam slid off his stool. His hands on her shoulders, he coaxed her to her feet. "The really smart ones work out or cry. Way I see it, crying's the cheapest route. No club fees, no bills to pay."

She wanted to laugh, but she couldn't. There was too much sadness in the way.

He had his arms around her now, and he was holding her to him. One human being offering comfort to another.

Though she felt that it was weak of her, Savannah couldn't help herself. She hadn't broken down when Aimee had been abducted, not even in the privacy of her own home. She'd been afraid that once she did, she wouldn't be able to pull the pieces together again.

Ever.

The closest she'd come was in the car earlier, but even then she'd managed to rally at the last moment.

But Sam, with his easy humor and his competent manner, made it so easy to lean on him. Made it too easy to stop being brave and strong, and just be afraid.

Surrendering, Savannah clung to him and cried quietly.

Sam held her for a long time, stroking her hair and just letting her cry herself out. He knew it was the best thing for her right now. That his heart twisted a little to hear her was beside the point. As was the fact that he felt something stirring inside him. All these things were extraneous.

But he couldn't quite get himself to believe it.

After a while, Savannah struggled to get hold of herself. She couldn't just dissolve this way. It wasn't fair to Sam.

Raising her face to his, she said, "You've got to stop being so nice."

He pretended to consider that. "I could kick you in the shin a couple of times if you like."

She felt her lips curving. "It might help."

It would also help, Sam thought, if he dropped his hands to his sides. Now.

But instead of dropping them, he found himself threading his fingers through her hair and framing her face. He wouldn't have been able to say later, if anyone had asked, how his lips came to be touching hers. Or just how he wound up kissing her.

All he could have said in his defense was that it

seemed—it *felt*—inevitable. Like the sun rising in the morning after a very long, dark night.

Savannah's pulse quickened as everything within her ran toward the light, toward the sweetness and comfort she felt in his kiss. She'd been strong all her life, but now she gravitated toward his strength, his kindness, like an empty vessel sorely in need of re-plenishing.

The kiss filled every corner of her being. And made her want more.

The flash of desire that came to her an instant later was a complete surprise. When she finally recognized it for what it was.

Savannah tightened her hands on his shoulders, fist-ing her fingers in his shirt and absorbing every nuance of the kiss like a starving shipwreck survivor finally faced with sustenance. Unable to justify her reaction, she just let it happen.

Sam felt his body pulsing in response to hers. Damn, what the hell did he think he was doing, kiss-ing her like this? Was he out of his mind? This was going against every rule he'd ever written for himself. And knowing that, admitting that, why the hell wasn't he pulling away?

The silent demand throbbed in Sam's mind almost as hard as his body throbbed in response to the woman in his arms.

It took more effort than he would ever have thought necessary to draw away from her.

Blowing out a breath, Sam looked down into her face: she looked dazed. Self-loathing pricked at his

conscience. How could he take advantage of her like
this?

"I'm sorry." The apology was a hoarse whisper.
"I shouldn't have done that."

She laid a finger to his lips to keep him from continuing. She didn't want to hear an apology. Not when
what he had done was tantamount to throwing her a
lifeline.

"Don't be. It's the nicest thing to have happened
to me since this whole ugly business started." *Maybe
even longer than that,* she thought.

Drawing away from him, Savannah self-con-
sciously ran a hand through her hair. She knew her
eyes had to be swollen from crying.

"I must look awful."

His eyes touched her softly, though he knew he had
no right to be feeling what he was feeling. Had no
right to have done what he'd done.

"Not that I can see."

She knew what she had to look like. Still, the compliment touched her. "I thought I was paying you to
be observant."

His eyes held hers. "You are."

This shouldn't have happened, Sam thought. No
way in hell was he supposed to kiss a client. He was
guilty of taking advantage of an emotionally vulnerable woman. He had nothing in his defense, no way
to absolve himself in his own eyes.

Still, he couldn't quite get himself to regret kissing
her. The most he could do was promise himself that
it wouldn't happen again. She didn't need a detective

who wasn't free to make a commitment complicating her life.

He saw her begin to clear away her plate. She hadn't touched the meal she'd made. He took it from her. "Why don't you see if you can get some rest?"

It was against her nature to leave things undone. She desperately needed order of some sort. Savannah looked at the frying pan in the sink. "The dishes—"

"I'll do them," he promised.

He was doing everything, she thought, this man that fate had pushed into her life: the dishes, answering the phone—

As if on cue, the telephone began to ring. Holding up a hand, Sam stopped her from answering it.

"I'll get it." His hand covered the receiver. "I'll wake you if it's anything," he promised.

She believed him, but she couldn't leave the room, tired as she was, until she knew who was on the other end of this call. Savannah held her breath as he picked up the receiver.

"King residence." He listened a moment, then covered the mouthpiece. Sam suppressed the frown. "It's George Cartwright. You want to talk to him?"

Exhaling, Savannah flushed, then held her hand out for the telephone. She wasn't certain exactly what she was feeling as she said "hello." *Confused* probably covered it best.

Trying to give her privacy, Sam turned his attention to the two plates on the counter. Hungrier than he first realized, he finished both meals quickly. There hadn't been that much there to begin with.

He slid both plates into the sink on top of the pan. It was impossible for him not to listen to the conversation. He told himself that listening was all right because what was being said might have something to do with the case, but he knew he was lying.

"No, really, George, there's nothing you can do. Not unless you know where she is. Thank you. I appreciate that. Yes, of course. Thank you—and good luck." Sam watched her hang up the phone.

He wanted to ask what she "appreciated," but he waited for her to volunteer the information.

She turned to face Sam, a bemused expression on her face. It had been more than six months since she'd heard from George. She'd never expected to again. Their parting hadn't been overly amicable. "George just wanted to offer me his support."

Sam nodded as he made short work of the dishes. He dried off his hands, disliking the feelings that were ricocheting through him. Feelings that had no business being there.

"Was he close to Aimee?"

"Close enough to think of her as a possible step-daughter. Not close enough to want to kidnap her." She was absolutely sure of that. "He was always very nice to her, but he wasn't overly attached. I was his primary interest, not Aimee. And no," she said before he had a chance to pose the question, "I don't think he'd kidnap her to get to me. There's someone else in his life now."

And she was happy for him. It was the reason he'd given for having hesitated about calling until now. But they had a history, however minor. And for old time's sake, George had asked her if she wanted him to come over. She'd turned him down. Maybe she wouldn't have if Sam hadn't been here. She was grateful to Sam for that, she realized. Grateful to him for not allowing her to possibly make a mistake because she felt so alone.

Whether he'd intended this or not, she didn't feel quite as alone anymore. She felt...felt things perhaps she shouldn't, she thought. Especially given the circumstances she found herself in. But there was something about the gentleness beneath his brash exterior, the kindnesses he extended when she least expected it, that broke through all her barriers, stirring the heart she'd been so sure was now just an empty shell.

The man did dishes, for heaven's sake. And there was something in his smile. Something reassuring and...

Abruptly, unwilling to let her thoughts stray further, she turned toward the linen closet. "Let me get you some bedding."

He saw no reason to go to any trouble. He'd been on more than his share of stakeouts. "That's okay, I don't need much."

She wouldn't push. "You're a rare man, Sam Walters." In more ways than one, she added silently.

"So they tell me." He smiled, making himself comfortable on the sofa. He made a mental note to have George Cartwright checked out. Just in case. "See you in the morning."

She left the room with his words ringing in her ears. Like everything else about him, they were oddly comforting.

Chapter 8

The smell of coffee, rich and aromatic, drew Sam out of the shallow sleep he'd succumbed to when the telephone had finally stopped ringing.

Moaning slightly as he stirred, eyes still shut, he reached for the telephone where he'd put it on the floor. It was only when his fingers had grasped the receiver that he realized the telephone wasn't ringing and that that wasn't what had woken him up.

Opening his eyes, the first thing Sam saw from his vantage point was a light gray skirt and a pair of very shapely legs. His brain, the fog only now lifting, told him that somehow the legs were connected to the coffee. It took him another minute or two before his memory caught up to him.

Sam sat bolt upright, a sheepish smile curving his

mouth as he looked up at Savannah. It wasn't his habit to be caught sleeping on the job.

"Sorry," he mumbled. "Didn't hear you come in."

Unable to lie in bed any longer, Savannah had been up and dressed for more than half an hour. When she'd passed the living room and looked in to find him asleep, she'd decided to make breakfast rather than wake him.

"I was trying to be quiet." She set the large blue mug in front of him on the coffee table. A thatch of dark blond hair was hanging in his eyes, and he looked more like a boy than a hardened private investigator. "You looked so comfortable, I was going to let you sleep."

He shook his head, dragging his hand through his hair and clearing away the last remnants of sleep from his system. Softly or not, he should have heard her walking in, he admonished himself.

"I do fine on seven minutes," he cracked. He'd had every intention of being up before she was. The sofa had proven to be way too comfortable. He eyed the dark liquid in the mug. A ray of sunlight was glancing off the surface. "As long as I have coffee."

Taking the mug in both hands, Sam brought it to his mouth and sipped almost reverently, like a man who'd been wandering the desert and was finally given something to clear his parched throat.

"God," he murmured after draining a third of the mug and feeling the coffee kick its way into his system, shaking it awake, "you're an angel of mercy."

She couldn't help smiling at his reaction. Apparently he'd been serious last night when he said he was easy to please.

"If all it takes is making coffee, I guess I qualify." She glanced toward the kitchen. "I made breakfast, too. Does that put me on the list for sainthood?" When he looked up at her, a pensive expression in his eyes, she lost her train of thought for a second. *Silly,* she chided silently. "It's just more eggs, with toast, but—"

Sam waved away her apology. Breakfast was usually a piece of bread, hardly toasted, on the run. If that.

"Coffee," he assured her. "I just need coffee and I'll be fine."

You didn't get a muscular build like that with just coffee, Savannah thought.

"You can't live on just coffee—" She stopped abruptly. At times, she was slow to pick up signals. She'd fed him last night. Maybe he didn't care for her cooking and was trying to be polite about it. "Unless of course you don't like eggs…"

Sam took another long swallow of coffee before answering. He was beginning to feel this side of human again.

"Eggs are fine." He focused on the wristwatch he always wore. It was a little after seven. "Wow, I didn't realize I slept in so late."

The term amused her. To most of the people she knew, sleeping in meant noon or thereabouts.

She'd done what he'd told her to last night: turned

off the telephone in her bedroom and tried to get some rest. Incredibly drained and exhausted, she'd tossed and turned, straining to listen for the ringing of the phone Sam had left on in the living room. She'd finally fallen into a fitful slumber.

Dream after dream had assaulted her. She'd spent the night searching for an endless parade of things that she'd lost, one after the other. Her purse, her keys, her car, her house. Each time she thought she found one, she'd lose something else. By morning, Savannah felt almost more exhausted than when she'd fallen asleep.

Stooping, she picked up the telephone and replaced it on the table behind the sofa. "When did the telephone stop ringing?"

Sam looked down at the notes he'd taken. He'd logged in each call, marking down the time and the number if it showed up on the LCD screen.

"About two-thirty." He saw the question in her eyes. "The last two calls were from insomniacs, wanting to know the latest details."

Savannah shivered. Those were the same kind of people who rubbernecked at accidents. "How can people be like that—so ghoulish?"

"There're a lot of crazies out there." He could testify to that firsthand. And to the converse as well. It was one of the things that kept him in this job instead of on a ranch somewhere in Wyoming. Tragedy brought out the best in most. "And a lot of nice people, too."

He drained the last of the coffee and looked regretfully at the empty mug. Megan could well take lessons from Savannah. "This is great stuff. Mind if I have some more?"

"No, of course not. I made plenty." Savannah began to take the mug from him, but instead, he rose to his feet still holding it.

"I'll just help myself."

"As you like." Savannah led the way.

Walking into the kitchen behind her, Sam paused to absorb the warm aroma. Her kitchen faced east, and the morning sun had come spilling into the room, brightening everything it touched. For a fleeting second, he was transported back to his childhood and Sunday mornings when his mother had insisted that the whole family sit down at the table for a hot breakfast.

It gave him a good feeling, remembering.

Refilling his mug, Sam took a seat at the counter. Savannah had set a place for him. Framed by two pieces of toast, sunny-side-up eggs waited on his pleasure. He felt his stomach pinching. Maybe he was hungry at that.

"If you don't mind, after breakfast I'm going to go over to my place to take a shower and get a change of clothes, then stop by the office to do a couple of things."

He wasn't going to lose her that easily. "What things?" Savannah asked as she slid onto the stool beside him, setting down another plate.

She'd made eggs for herself as well, mainly to keep Sam company when he ate. But she had no more of an appetite now than she had had last night. She'd lost three pounds since Aimee had been kidnapped. If this kept up, when they found Aimee, Savannah figured she was going to have to get a whole new wardrobe. Or start drinking milk shakes three times a day.

Aimee loved milk shakes, she thought fondly. Her throat tightened. Savannah looked at Sam, waiting for an answer.

"I want to make more copies of that photograph the saleswoman IDed, and pass them around." Megan's younger brother, Rusty, was always looking to earn a little extra money when he wasn't attending classes at the university. He could pay Rusty to canvas the area with the photograph, ask some of the residents who lived just beyond the mall if they'd seen a little girl dressed like that around. "I thought I'd also post that photograph on the Internet."

He was talking about something that was second nature to her, but right now, she was drawing a blank. "The Internet? Are you talking about setting up a site for Aimee?"

He finished his meal. "I don't have to. There's already an entire site devoted to missing kids. It's called the Missing and Exploited Children National Center." The site had been set up several years ago by the government agency of the same name located in Arlington, Virginia. The database was crammed with information that was periodically updated. Photographs were even age-altered when enough time had passed. "The police tap into it regularly to help them track down missing kids." He didn't want her dwelling on the fact that there were huge numbers of children reported missing every year, or how Aimee could be found given odds like that. Currently, he knew, there were more than six-thousand active cases. It was a daunting figure. "I figure it won't hurt to have the altered photograph posted there."

As he spoke, another idea came to him. "We can also have it shown on the news." He'd give Gretchen a call as soon as he got into the office. Gretchen was his brother-in-law's sister, and she was a reporter on one of the local television stations. This would be right up her alley. "I know a reporter who'll be happy to broadcast it on the evening news. If that doesn't work, we could ask your father to talk to his friends and get it on the air that way."

He had to get rolling. But as he stood up, he saw that short of breaking up the yolks on her plate, Savannah hadn't touched her food. He remembered that she hadn't eaten anything last night, either. Or during the course of the day before.

Sam frowned. She couldn't keep this up. "You know, if you don't start eating something, by the time I do find Aimee, I'm going to have to bring her to the hospital in order to see you. You'll have tubes running through you and they'll be feeding you intravenously. You want Aimee to see you like that?"

"No." She had no idea that he had this dramatic streak. "I'm just not hungry."

"Eat anyway." He watched her stare at the plate. Savannah made no effort to pick up a fork. The lady was nothing if not stubborn. "Eat or I won't take you with me." It sounded like a childish threat, but it was all the leverage he had available.

Ordinarily, she would have bristled at having an ultimatum thrown at her. But there was something in his voice, a kind note buried in the stern order, that had her smiling despite herself.

She picked up her fork and went through the motions. "Are you always such a mother hen?"

"Nope, I can honestly say this is a first." It was. So was losing control and kissing a client, he thought ruefully.

Moving away from the counter, Sam took his plate to the sink. As he rinsed it off, he glanced in her direction. And smiled. She was eating. One point for his team. "You're a bad influence on me," he added.

Whatever she was going to say in response was instantly forgotten as the telephone's shrill ring pushed everything else into the background.

Sam sighed, turning off the water. "Looks like they're getting an early start." He wiped his hands on the back of his jeans as the phone rang a second time. "Maybe we should just let your machine get that."

The answering machine had been full when they'd come in last night. Sam had used up the lull between incoming calls by playing the tape and listening to the various messages. It was an exercise in futility. People had called to ask questions, or give advice. A few promised to pray. No one said anything useful.

Savannah couldn't listen to the telephone ring the

allotted number of times before the machine picked up. Turning on the stool, she reached for the wall phone and pulled the receiver to her.

Her heart sped up as she said, "Hello?"

"Is this Mrs. King?" The voice on the other end belonged to a woman. There was a slight accent that Savannah couldn't immediately place.

"This is Savannah King." Savannah didn't bother correcting the salutation. One of the first calls she'd taken was from a woman who'd told her that God was punishing her for being an unwed mother by taking her daughter away. She didn't need to go through anything like that again.

"Put it on speakerphone," Sam mouthed, coming up next to her.

Savannah pressed down the extreme right-hand button, and the tiny light above it glowed red. The woman's voice, strong and courtly, filled the space between them as Savannah replaced the receiver.

"Savannah, my name is Eliza Eldridge. I've just had a dream about your daughter."

Sam exchanged looks with Savannah. Another crazy wanting to pass the time of day. Curbing his anger, Sam reached over to terminate the connection, but Savannah caught his hand. She shook her head urgently when he looked at her in silent query. She wanted to hear this. Wanted to hear everything, because somehow, someway, something had to make sense eventually. Something had to lead her to her daughter.

"I'm clairvoyant," the woman told her. "Before

The Editor's "Thank You" Free Gifts Include:

- ● Two BRAND-NEW romance novels!
- ● An exciting mystery gift!

PLACE FREE GIFT SEAL HERE

YES! I have placed my Editor's "Thank You" seal in the space provided above. Please send me 2 free books and a fabulous mystery gift. I understand I am under no obligation to purchase any books, as explained on the back and on the opposite page.

345 SDL CQUV

245 SDL CQUK
(S-IM-06/99)

Name:

PLEASE PRINT

Address: Apt.#:

City:

State/
Prov.:   Postal
                                    Zip/Code:

Thank You!

DETACH AND MAIL CARD TODAY!

The Silhouette Reader Service™ — Here's how it works:

Accepting your 2 free books and mystery gift places you under no obligation to buy anything. You may keep the books and gift and return the shipping statement marked "cancel." If you do not cancel, about a month later we'll send you 6 additional novels and bill you just $3.57 each in the U.S., or $3.96 each in Canada, plus 25¢ delivery per book and applicable taxes if any.* That's the complete price and — compared to the cover price of $4.25 in the U.S. and $4.75 in Canada — it's quite a bargain! You may cancel at any time, but if you choose to continue, every month we'll send you 6 more books, which you may either purchase at the discount price or return to us and cancel your subscription.

*Terms and prices subject to change without notice. Sales tax applicable in N.Y. Canadian residents will be charged applicable provincial taxes and GST.

If offer card is missing write to: The Silhouette Reader Service, 3010 Walden Ave., P.O. Box 1867, Buffalo, NY 14240-1867

BUSINESS REPLY MAIL
FIRST-CLASS MAIL   PERMIT NO. 717   BUFFALO, NY

POSTAGE WILL BE PAID BY ADDRESSEE

SILHOUETTE READER SERVICE
3010 WALDEN AVE
PO BOX 1867
BUFFALO NY 14240-9952

NO POSTAGE
NECESSARY
IF MAILED
IN THE
UNITED STATES

you hang up, I want you to know that I don't have a little storefront shop where I tell people's fortunes. And I don't have a 900 number where I pretend to delve into people's souls by telling them bland generalities. But I do see things. Not always, and not on call. And sometimes I'm wrong."

The woman's voice was soft, kind, and there was a peacefulness to it that seemed to weave its way into Savannah, urging her to listen.

"But last night," Eliza went on, "I had a dream about your daughter. It was so strong, I had to call."

Yeah, right, thought Sam. The woman was a con artist, looking to make something off Savannah's misery. Sam struggled to hold his temper.

"What sort of a dream?" he demanded.

"Is that your private investigator with you, Savannah?" Eliza asked.

The question drove a chill down Savannah's back. She glanced at Sam. How had the woman known?

"Yes," Savannah answered guardedly. "Now tell me about your dream."

She knew that she was setting herself up, and yet she couldn't help listening. Couldn't help hoping that Eliza Eldridge was the genuine article.

"I was walking by a man-made lake," Eliza began. "There were ducks swimming on the water, and there were some children feeding them."

"Was Aimee with them?" It was an absurd question, Savannah realized. And yet...

"No, she wasn't." Eliza measured out her words. This wasn't easy. "There was somebody out on a boat—fishing, I think. And there were townhouses in the background, not far from the water.''

Savannah's mouth went dry. She recognized the description. The woman was talking about Windwalker Lake. It wasn't located too far from her office. She'd gone there with Aimee less than a month ago. Aimee loved to feed the ducks that made their home on the lake.

''Go on,'' Savannah urged breathlessly.

Sam listened in silence, ninety-nine percent certain that this was some sort of hoax. But the expression on Savannah's face was beginning to arouse some doubts in his mind.

''I didn't exactly see your daughter,'' Eliza confessed. ''It was more as if I 'felt' her, felt her presence when I came to the edge of the lake.'' She paused, uncertain how to phrase this next part.

''Yes?'' Savannah fought to keep her voice from going up.

''I came to the edge of the lake,'' Eliza repeated. ''And when I looked down, there was a pair of pink-and-white checkered sneakers on the bank, and a trail of blood leading into the water.''

Savannah covered her mouth to keep the scream from escaping.

Sam jerked up the telephone receiver, silencing the speaker connection. His first reaction was to tell the woman to go to hell and leave Savannah alone. But he knew that Savannah—at least a part of Savannah—believed the woman. That part would have no peace until this was checked out. So he kept his temper and his cool, and gave Eliza instructions instead.

"Look, lady, if you're on the level, I want you to meet me at the Newport Beach police station in half an hour. Ask for Detective Underwood—"

Eliza interrupted him. "That's not you."

He wasn't sure just what kind of a trick was being played here, but it *was* a trick. Wasn't it?

"No, that's not me. And you don't have to try to impress me. For now, I'll grant that *you* think you know something." He glanced at Savannah's pale face. "So we'll check out your 'vision,' or whatever it is you want to call it." He figured Underwood had the manpower and resources to do that better than he did.

So much for a shower and a change of clothes, he realized. He hoped Cade hadn't gotten attached to this particular pair of pants and shirt.

The woman on the other end wasn't saying anything. "Are you willing to do that?" He half expected her to make up an excuse.

"Yes, Mr. Walters, I'm willing to do that. I'll be there."

"Good, so will I." It was as good as a warning.

It was only when he hung up the receiver that it occurred to Sam that at no time had he given the woman his name.

But he didn't have time to dwell on that. The look in Savannah's eyes reflected sheer terror.

"Oh God, Sam, what if it's true? What if she actually 'sees' this? What if Aimee's really—" Savannah couldn't bring herself to say it. Saying it would make it somehow true.

He took hold of her shoulders, as if the very act could anchor her to reality.

"Listen to me, Savannah. Ninety-nine times out of a hundred, these people are just talking through their hats—even if they're convinced they're quoting Revelations."

She knew he was right, and yet she couldn't shake this dreadful feeling. "But you *are* checking it out, aren't you?"

"Yes, but only because there's nothing else to go on right now." He wished there was some kind of lead, *any* kind of lead. But there was nothing but this to work with. Sam looked into her eyes, willing Savannah to believe him. "Aimee's not in that lake, do you hear me? She's alive."

"Alive," Savannah echoed.

Gulping in a shaky breath, she managed to calm down a little. It vaguely registered in the back of her mind that she was relying for support on a man who was almost a stranger. It should have bothered her. She had no idea why it didn't. Instead, she was grateful that he was in her life.

"Okay, let's go."

Underwood looked from Sam and Savannah to the petite, dark-haired woman who had shaken up Savannah's world with a single phone call. His expression testified to the doubts he had. In spades.

Eliza Eldridge had come to the police station armed

with letters that were signed by law enforcement officials and a scrapbook of yellowing newspaper articles trapped behind clear plastic sheets.

A couple of calls to verify the letters had gone a long way in changing his initial opinion that she was a crackpot. According to some very influential people, the lady was what she claimed to be. A true clairvoyant.

A recent transplant from Fort Worth, Texas, Eliza had a "gift" that winked in and out of her life and that, at times, the police had found useful. She'd led them to missing children before.

Or so a skillful reporter might want them to believe, Underwood thought, looking at the scrapbook. He could see by the look on Sam's face that the other man felt the same way he did about so-called clairvoyants.

Underwood handed the scrapbook back to Eliza. "I don't believe in things that can't be scientifically proven, Ms. Eldridge."

Eliza was accustomed to skeptics. She wasn't out to convert the world. Only to help when she could.

"Do you believe in hunches, Detective Underwood?" she asked mildly.

Ben's frown deepened. Though he didn't believe that she had any sort of tangible abilities, he wasn't about to waste time debating her, either. He had a very strong hunch in this case that the lady could more than adequately handle herself in that department.

The bottom line was finding the little girl. That

meant ruling out all possible theories, one by one. Even ones that were off the wall.

"I got the department to okay three divers for three hours," Ben told Sam. "That's the best I can do."

"It's a relatively small lake," Sam said. "That should be more than enough time to cover the area." He looked at Savannah. "And to prove that Aimee's not down there."

Savannah's hand tightened around his.

Savannah was peripherally aware of Sam's hand holding hers. She wasn't sure just how tightly she was squeezing it. Her eyes were fixed on the lake. Each time one of the divers broke through the surface, she felt as if her heart stopped beating.

But each time, there was nothing in the diver's arms, and she sighed with relief. And her heart would begin beating again.

Savannah didn't know how much more of this she could take.

Underwood looked at his watch. There wasn't much time left on the clock. Standing beside Sam, the police detective looked at Eliza. The woman stood apart from them, stoically watching the divers. It seemed to Underwood that there was more than just distance separating them. There was an aura about Eliza, something that caused him to feel respectful of the woman rather than cynically dismissing her.

Sam could feel his fingers turning numb. He inclined his head toward Savannah's. She hadn't moved since the scuba divers had first gone into the lake.

"Time's almost up," he told her.

"And they didn't find her." Every whispered syllable was wrapped in relief.

"And they're not going to," Underwood stated.

Though he tried to divorce himself from the personal aspect of the cases he worked—much the way he knew Sam did—Ben couldn't help feeling sorry for Savannah. The woman had to be going through hell.

"Why don't you take her home?" Ben suggested to Sam.

Coming to, Savannah shook her head. "Not home." After being subjected to this, she'd only climb the walls if she was alone. Suddenly aware that she was still holding Sam's hand, Savannah released it. "You said you wanted to stop at your apartment and then go to the office. Take me with you."

It seemed somehow callous to turn her down.

"Okay." Sam saw the divers coming out of the lake. "Let's wrap this up."

Ben put his hand on Sam's shoulder and shook his head. "My divers. I get to say when they wrap it up." Then, with a flicker of a grin, he called over to his men. "Wrap it up, boys." It was then that Eliza turned from the lake and came over to join them. "Ms. Eldridge, I'm happy to say that this time, you're wrong."

"Not as happy as I am, Detective. Not nearly as happy as I am." She shifted her deep blue eyes to Savannah and placed her hand over hers. "I'm so sorry to have put you through this. But the dream was very vivid. If there was any chance…''

Savannah nodded. The woman had been sincere in her call. She didn't blame her.

''I understand.''

''I'll keep a good thought,'' Eliza called after her, as Sam ushered Savannah away to his car.

They were going to need a lot more than just good thoughts, Sam thought. And soon.

Chapter 9

Savannah felt dazed as she got into Sam's car. Dazed and numb.

The numbness melted in the heat of a dozen emotions that pushed their way forward, crowding her mind, her soul. She felt like laughing and crying at the same time.

Aimee wasn't at the bottom of the lake.

There was still hope.

But where *was* she?

Frustration began to gnaw away at the relief. Needing something to fill the air, she leaned forward and turned up the music in the car.

"You can change it if you like," Sam told her. He liked the oldies, songs from two and three decades ago, but he knew that not everyone was partial to them. His brothers thought he was crazy to find anything that came before the current decade even mildly entertaining.

Savannah shook her head at the offer. "No, I like this kind of music."

Sam glanced toward her as he took a right. The lady was trying very hard to be strong, but even steel cracked under certain conditions. If he made a left at the next light, he could still drive by her house without going that much out of his way.

"Are you sure you don't want me to take you home?"

"No." She had to be out, doing something. Staying in the house and listening to the telephone ring would make her crazy.

He could understand her not wanting to be alone right now. "Or to your parents' house?"

She laughed shortly. Her parents both felt terrible about this, but they hadn't a single clue how to react to her. She didn't need to feel awkward on top of everything else. She needed to feel useful.

She needed, she thought, to be with Sam.

"A definite no." Savannah looked at him. Was he thinking of telling her that she couldn't come along after all? "I told you, I'm willing to pay you more if—"

For all intents and purposes, he was in her employ, but it irked him to have his position in her life reduced to dollars and cents.

"And I said it wasn't a matter of money." He realized he'd bitten that off a little more tersely than he'd intended. He supposed he was feeling edgy, too.

Despite what he'd said to Savannah, a part of him had believed—had been afraid—that they would find Aimee's body at the bottom of the lake. "Right now, it's a matter of not having a possible hysterical woman on my hands."

The defensiveness she felt was way out of proportion, and she knew it, even as she demanded, "Have I gotten hysterical yet?"

He spared her a long look before answering. "No, not yet."

That sounded as if he was counting the minutes until it happened. "And I won't." It was a solemn promise she made to herself as well as to him.

"I'm only thinking of you."

He didn't want her subjected to any more of this than she had to be. If he could have found a way, he would have spared her the last four hours. For that matter, he would have fielded the phone call from Eliza if he'd been able.

"Well, don't. Just think of Aimee. I can take care of myself." Her angry words crowded out the music coming from the radio.

Savannah stared out the window. Her conscience caught up to her before they reached the next light. She wasn't accustomed to having someone care about how she felt. Wasn't accustomed, she realized, to a man like Sam. Able, considerate, and dangerously attractive, Sam Walters was like no one else she'd ever met. If her emotions weren't tied up in little knots, she would have acknowledged the fact a lot sooner. He didn't deserve the way she'd just treated him.

Savannah blew out a long breath. Her cheeks still flushed. "I'm sorry," she apologized. "I didn't mean to jump all over you."

She thought she detected a glimmer of a smile on his lips, but Sam kept his face forward.

"Don't worry about it. I've put up with a hell of a lot worse than what you just said to me. If it makes you feel any better and you want to blow off some steam, you go right ahead. Yell at me."

"No, I'm done." Savannah folded her hands in her lap. "I'll be good."

She would be, too, he thought, his mind straying again.

He'd better hurry up to that cold shower, Sam counseled himself. Otherwise, he was liable to be in a whole lot of trouble.

The sudden, shrill ringing coming from her purse had Savannah jumping a good inch off her seat, despite the seat belt that restrained her. Her response almost made him swerve into the next lane. He righted the wheel in time to avoid hitting a blue sedan.

He'd had about all the excitement he wanted to endure for one day, and it wasn't much past noon yet. Sam spared her as long a look as he dared. "You okay?"

Chagrined, Savannah shrugged vaguely as she dug through her purse.

"I forgot I still had my cell phone with me."

She found it and she flipped it open. It amazed her that the battery was still working. She'd forgotten all about recharging it last night. She used it predominantly to keep in touch with her office, and to be available to the baby-sitter she employed to stay with Aimee when she had to work outside the house.

She had no idea who would be calling her now.

"Hello?"

"How are you holding up, Savannah?"

Savannah felt some of the tension leave her body as the familiar voice registered. *Elliott.* She should have known.

"As well as can be expected, Elliott. Thanks for asking."

"Hey, what are friends for? I called your house this morning, but you were gone. I was worried about you," he explained.

The more she thought about it, the more Elliott seemed like the big brother she never had. Her parents hadn't even called to see how she was this morning. They were undoubtedly afraid that she would tell them, and then they wouldn't know what to say.

"I'm fine, Elliott. We—" Unable to continue for a moment, Savannah licked her bottom lip, looking for words to describe what she'd just been through.

The small, almost undetectable movement of her tongue along her lips caught Sam's eye. And his imagination. He tried not to let it distract him, but it took effort. A lot of effort.

Sam forced his mind back to the conversation, at least what he could glean from her end of it. It seemed odd to Sam that a married man would pay this much attention to a woman, and not have some ulterior motive.

Not simon-pure like you, huh, Sam? he mocked himself silently.

Savannah tried again. "We got a call early this morning from a clairvoyant."

"We?"

"Sam—the man I hired to find Aimee," she explained, "and I. The woman dreamed that Aimee'd drowned. That her body was at the bottom of a lake."

"No!" The single word, drenched in anguish, rang in her ear. And then, there was nothing. She thought that she had lost the connection.

"Elliott, are you still there?"

"Don't let those cranks make you believe that, Savannah," Elliott said finally. "Aimee's not dead."

She appreciated the strength she heard in his voice, and appreciated that he believed so strongly that her daughter was alive. It helped her hang on to her own belief.

"It's all right," Savannah told him. For a moment, she felt as if she were comforting him, as if he were the one whose daughter was in jeopardy. Because he loved his own daughter so much, he was probably identifying with what she was going through. "Sam and Detective Underwood had divers check out the area that the psychic saw in her dream. They didn't find Aimee."

"Of course they didn't. She's not at the bottom of some lake. She's alive. I know she is."

He was angry for her, Savannah thought. His friendship meant a great deal to her.

"Are you sure there isn't anything I can do for you?" Elliott asked again.

"No, really." Savannah realized that she was shaking inside, and tried to compose herself. She ran her hand over her eyes. "Oh Elliott, if there was just some way I could know that she was still alive. I close my eyes, wishing for a sign, something. This not knowing—it's hell."

"I know. I really, really wish you didn't have to go through this, Savannah. I want you to know that. I only wish…" His voice trailed off, and she was touched by the emotion she heard in it.

"I know." She could guess what he was wishing. The same thing she was: that Aimee was back. "Thank you. Elliott, I'm going to hang up now. I know this sounds silly, but I want to keep all lines clear."

"Sure, sure. I understand. Just hang in there. I know she's all right. Everyone here is so concerned that I've got you on speakerphone so you won't have to repeat this story. And they send their love." As if on cue, Savannah heard several other voices chime in, reinforcing Elliott's sentiments. "Take care, Savannah. I'll call again soon."

"'Bye." She heard a chorus of goodbyes in response. Savannah closed the case and then pressed it against her lips, thinking. "I wish I was."

"You wish you were…what?" The call had generated more than one question in Sam's head.

For a moment, she'd almost forgotten that she wasn't alone in the car. Savannah dropped the cell phone into her purse. "Elliott said he knew she was alive. I only wish I was as convinced as he was."

Could be just a good friend being supportive, Sam thought.

But she wasn't paying him to rubber-stamp her impressions. She was paying him to investigate, to probe. That meant shaking every tree he came in contact with.

"How long have you known Elliott?"

"Six years." Didn't he remember that? "I already told you—"

Savannah turned to look at him. Suddenly, she realized where he was going with his questions. She refused to allow Sam to take her there. Her world had been cracked open; she couldn't let him siphon away all the trust as well. She needed to believe in someone, in at least one friend.

"Oh, no, not Elliott. You can't take that away from me. You can't make me not trust him, too." If she became suspicious of her friends, paranoia would be waiting in the wings to embrace her. "That won't leave me anyone—except for my parents and sister."

"And me," he pointed out.

"And you," she echoed. "But that goes without saying."

Yeah, he thought, it did. A lot of things went without saying. And maybe, in the long run, it was better that way. For both of them.

"I'm not trying to get you not to trust him. I'm just trying to get a clearer picture."

"Of Elliott?"

Since she was sensitive about the subject, he replied tactfully, "Of everyone. I just find it a little unusual for a married man to take such an interest in a single woman."

"I told you, we're friends. Our daughters are friends." She paused, debating, then added, "And sometimes he cries on my shoulder."

"How wet are the tears?"

"It's not what you think." She felt herself growing defensive. Sam probably thought Elliott was one of those men who used the old my-wife-doesn't-understand-me line. "He asks my advice about his wife. Sometimes he feels that there's no pleasing her—and he really wants to," she emphasized. "Look, I don't know about the kind of men in your world, but Elliott's not like that."

"Okay, you've convinced me."

He didn't look convinced. "What does this have to do with Aimee's disappearance?"

"I don't know yet. Maybe nothing. Probably nothing," he amended. "But I won't know until I figure out what does."

"Can you make it any clearer than that?"

He only wished he could. Sam shook his head. "Not at the moment."

"Who are all these people?"

Savannah's question floated back to Sam from his

cluttered living room. Barefoot and shirtless, Sam came out of his equally cluttered bedroom to see.

He grinned when he saw where she was standing. Just off the living room, in a space that was more of an indentation than an alcove and that laughingly served as his home office, was a wall that was covered with framed photographs of varying sizes and shapes.

"That's my rogue's gallery." He saw her raise an eyebrow. "Those are my nephews and my niece."

He was standing very close to her. Close enough for Savannah to feel the heat emanating from his body. Or was that hers? The woman on the radio had predicted record-breaking temperatures today, and it felt to Savannah as if Sam's apartment had a head start.

Savannah forced herself to turn away and looked at the display on his wall. Across the top were photographs of five boys ranging from about two to fifteen. A single girl was placed between them. They were all smiling. Two of the boys had grins like Sam's, she realized.

"Somehow, I can't picture you with a family."

That made two of them, he thought. "Technically, it's not mine," he reminded her. "It's borrowed. They belong to my brothers and sister." A warmth entered his voice, the way it always did when he talked about his extended family. "I have to put them back after I finish playing with them."

Savannah turned to look at him. "Do you?"

The moment hung between them. He knew he wanted to kiss her again. Knew he couldn't. To keep from pulling her into his arms, he shoved his hands into his back pockets. "Do I what?"

"Play with them?" With no effort at all, she could visualize him on the floor, playing with the smallest ones. Teasing his niece. Palling around with his oldest nephew. It was funny how she could sense that about him, despite his rough and tough exterior.

"Figure of speech," he brushed off. And then a grin came to call him a liar. "Yeah, I do. They tell me I play make-believe better than their parents." He tried not to make that sound like he was bragging, but a note of pride betrayed him. "Probably has something to do with my job. I have to be inventive on the spur of the moment. Kids like that."

And they could also sense when someone was being genuine with them. She'd learned that quickly enough on her own. Children had a wonderful ability to see right into your heart.

"So why don't you have any kids of your own?" she wanted to know. "You obviously like them."

"Yes, I like them. I think kids are great." They had an innocence that he held in awe. Even Richie, who was going on fifteen and thought he was so cool, was still innocent when it came to the darker side of the world. "But I don't have any kids for the same reason I don't have a wife. Because they wouldn't fit into this kind of a life."

What was he doing, he thought, standing here half-naked, having this conversation with a woman who could easily get under his skin if he let her? Sam began to walk away.

"How do you know until you try—or did you?"

Her question pulled him back. He turned around again. "No, I didn't. But my father did. Seemed to me like every big occasion that came up, he was missing. On the job. I wondered about it as a kid. Thought maybe it had something to do with me. After a while, I accepted it." Or made peace with it as best he could, Sam thought. He never really stopped wishing his father was there. It was what had led him to his decision. "I don't want to be that kind of a father to my kids. A father who's not there for the important moments in their lives.

"But I love doing what I'm doing, so…" His voice trailed off, leaving Savannah to draw the obvious conclusion.

She surprised him by asking, "Did you love your father?"

Yeah, he loved him. That was why it hurt so much when he wasn't there. Sam shrugged casually. "Sure."

Savannah tried not to notice the way the muscles in his chest rippled when he moved his shoulders like that. "And he loved you."

Memories crowded in, tiny precious gems winking in and out of his brain. "Yeah, he loved me." There was no question in his mind.

"I'd think that would be all that mattered," she said. "That he loved you. If he got that message across, then he was a good father. You'd probably be a good one, too," she finished, resting her case. It wasn't much of a leap. More of a skip, she thought.

"Oh?" He couldn't help the amusement that came into his voice. She was turning the tables on him. He was the one who was supposed to make rapid assessments, not her. "And what makes you think that?"

"I heard you with your nephew the other day when he called about his birthday party, remember? You could have brushed him off." A lot of other men would have. Her father had always made her feel that she took a back seat to his work as well as to his friends.

There was no point debating a hypothetical point. He'd made up his mind about the path his life would take a long time ago. It was mapped out, and there was no reason to have that map redrafted.

He looked down at her face and felt something stirring again. Something that, if he were being honest with himself, really hadn't stopped stirring since he'd kissed her last night. Maybe even before then.

Sam's palms itched. He wanted to touch her, to feel her skin. To feel her against him. He was acutely aware of her, acutely aware of the feelings that were twisting inside him.

The better part of valor was knowing when to retreat. And Valor was his middle name.

Sam backed away from her. Away from the mistake he was about to make if he remained standing within a heartbeat of her.

"I'd better go take my shower."

Only when he left the room did Savannah realize that she was holding her breath.

She let it go.

* * *

To occupy her mind, she'd asked him all sorts of questions about his extended family, as he drove them to his office less than forty minutes later.

Grateful for a neutral topic, Sam told her their names and ages, their hobbies, and a few anecdotes about them.

As they talked, Sam began to see why people were so drawn to Savannah. When the sadness in her eyes abated even marginally, there was something bright and compelling in them. In her entire manner.

Something that made a person want to open up to her and be in her light.

The thought almost made him laugh out loud. He was waxing poetic. Sam Walters, the man who had almost flunked high school English the semester they had to tackle all that "dumb poetry," as he'd called it then. He found it rather amazing.

But amazing or not, he couldn't allow this to happen. Couldn't allow himself to think of Savannah as other than a client, a woman in need who had come to him to find her child. Anything else was out of the question. And unethical.

It was hard keeping that uppermost in his mind when the sun insisted on tangling in her hair as they drove down Pacific Coast Highway to his office.

Cade and Megan were both out of the office when Sam arrived with Savannah. He'd planned to touch base with them, but he could do that later if he really needed to. He left a note for Megan to see if she could pull up anything on George Cartwright. And maybe Elliott Reynolds.

The one person he did need to see was in the office.

Glancing up from the report she was typing, Alex looked surprised to see him walk in.

"Alex, can you get me Rusty on the telephone?"

Miniaturizing the window with the report she was typing, Alex pulled up the list of telephone numbers she had stored. She jotted down the one she needed.

"Megan said something about his taking summer school classes," Sam said.

"He's a student?" Savannah asked. She thought the agency only employed professionals.

"Rusty is Megan's younger brother. He's in his last year at UCI," Sam told her. "Criminology. Wants to follow in his big sister's footsteps, except he won't come out and say it." Taking the number from Alex, he winked at Savannah as he walked past her into his office. "It's a macho thing."

The small flutter that suddenly materialized in the pit of her stomach caught Savannah entirely by surprise. She pressed her hand against her stomach, as if to rub away its existence.

It lingered a moment anyway.

With his back to her, Sam quickly pressed the numbers on the keypad. He heard the line being picked up on the third ring. He kept his fingers crossed that it wasn't an answering machine.

It wasn't.

"Hey, Rusty, how's it going?"

He paused as he listened to the young man on the

other end. He'd known Rusty since before Rusty could shave. The image remained embedded in his mind despite the fact that Rusty was now well over six-two, with the kind of brawny frame bodybuilders pined for.

"Got a class today? Oh? When?" Sam paused, listening. The time was right. "Good, how'd you like to do a little legwork for me? Yes, I'll pay you—" Sam laughed "—although you could think of it as on-the-job training. Get your tail on over here as fast as you can." He glanced at Savannah before adding, "We're pressed for time."

She waited until he hung up before asking, "What is it you want him to do?"

"Canvas the development right behind the mall. Maybe someone was walking their dog at the right time, or watering their rosebushes, or washing their car on the driveway. Or just staring out a window. We keep asking until we get an answer from someone."

Sam sat down at his desk and turned on his computer, unconsciously waiting for the familiar notes it gave off when it was ready for use.

"You might want to get comfortable." He indicated the chair behind her. "This might take a while," he warned. "I don't type very fast."

Finally, something she could do. Savannah was at his elbow.

"Get up." It came out as more of an order than she'd intended. Sam looked at her quizzically. "This is my field. Tell me what you want."

He swallowed the answer that rose to his lips. But he thought it nonetheless as he got up and gave her his seat.

You.

Chapter 10

Taking the seat that Sam had just vacated, Savannah was immediately aware of the warmth that caressed her limbs as she sat down. His warmth. The sensation seeped into her system, jolting her as it carved out a place for itself.

Other than when he had kissed her that one time, Sam had made no moves toward her. Instead of behaving like a predatory male, the way some men she knew had done, he'd been nothing but courteous and thoughtful. She deeply appreciated the fact that though Sam Walters was as good-looking as they came, he was not full of himself. He'd been exactly what she needed: a supportive male who didn't crowd her.

From the outside, the relationship between them all seemed very aboveboard, very cut-and-dried.

And yet it wasn't.

She could feel something between them. A quiet sizzle that was evident when he so much as touched her elbow, or looked at her a certain way. It was in his words and in his expression. And in the way she reacted to them.

To him.

For the most part, she'd sworn off any sort of relationships with men since Jarred had boarded the plane for England and flown out of her life. Having given him her heart, only to have it thoughtlessly tossed back to her after the affair was over, she'd found that she had nothing left to give anyone else. She'd tried to build something with George purely because she'd felt that she had to give Aimee a father, a balanced life.

It was doomed to failure from the start, because while she had the utmost respect and a measure of affection for George, she couldn't bring herself to go through with the wedding. She didn't love him. Didn't feel that strange tingling, down-to-her-toes electrical sensation the way she had with Jarred.

The way she did at this moment.

This was ridiculous, Savannah chided herself. She was just being vulnerable—and maybe even just a little needy. It wounded her pride to admit it, but she needed someone in her life to hold her hand, and Sam was holding it.

She was paying him to do that, she reminded herself. And since it was for pay, it wasn't the kind of thing to base a relationship on.

Banking down any further thoughts on the subject, and forcing herself to block the warm sensation penetrating the backs of her thighs, Savannah scooted the chair closer to the desk. She cleared her throat as she looked up at Sam.

"What do you want me to type?" she asked.

The look in his eyes broke through miles of barriers she'd erected for herself. Savannah took a deep breath and waited.

Sam recited the proper Internet address for the Missing and Exploited Children National Center. He knew it by heart, and wished he didn't. Wished that there was no need for a site like that to even exist. In a perfect world, there wouldn't be. But he'd known since he was eleven years old that the world was far from perfect.

As the accessed site came into focus on the monitor screen, the blood from Savannah's face felt as if it were drained away.

Hitting the scroll button, she saw name after name. Picture after picture. So many missing children. How were they ever going to find just one?

How were they ever going to find Aimee?

Sam could read her mind as easily as if the thought had been written in ten-inch letters on a huge chalkboard set up in front of him.

He laid a hand on her shoulder and squeezed. "We'll find her, Savannah. Children on that board get found every day."

And some never do. The haunting thought throbbed in her brain.

The positive side—she had to remember to focus on the positive side, she thought fiercely. "Tell me what you want me to write."

Hearing a knock at the door to his office, Sam glanced at his watch. He knew exactly how long it took to get here from Rusty's apartment under favorable traffic conditions. Rusty had shaved corners off the record. He wondered if somewhere there were traffic tickets with Rusty's name on them.

"What took you so long?" he cracked.

Rusty tucked his helmet under his arm. He looked more like a squeaky-clean, would-be astronaut, than someone who rode a motorcycle.

"I decided to take the scenic route." His eyes slid appreciatively toward the woman at Sam's computer. It occurred to him that he knew her from somewhere. Her face teased his mind, eluding recognition. "What've you got for me?" he asked Sam.

Sam had always liked Rusty's eagerness. The uncomplicated boy had grown up to be an uncomplicated, open man. It had to be nice not to have any baggage to carry around.

Russell Andreini had been called Rusty all his life despite several sporadic attempts on his part to get people to call him Russell, or at least Russ. His sister Megan had christened him Rusty when he was three days old, and the name had stuck. He no longer resented it. It wasn't in his nature to resent anything for more than a few moments at most. He was as easygoing as his sister was quick-tempered. Together, his mother had once said, they made the perfect person. He never thought to disagree.

Long before Megan had joined ChildFinders, Inc., and ever since Rusty had devoured his first Sherlock Holmes novel at the age of ten, the boy had wanted to become a private investigator. When Megan had become part of the agency, he'd volunteered his services time and again until Cade had finally taken him up on it. Nowadays, they called on him regularly.

Pulling a scratch pad closer to him on the desk, Sam wrote down the name of the residential development that hugged the northern perimeter of the outdoor mall where Aimee had disappeared. He handed the sheet to Rusty, then gave him a copy of the altered photograph.

"I want you to knock on a few doors and see if anyone saw this child last Thursday morning around eleven a.m. or thereabouts."

Stuffing the paper into his back pocket, Rusty studied the face in the photograph. Another missing kid. He couldn't begin to understand the type of monster who would rip a child away from everyone they knew. But then, he didn't have to understand, he just had to stop them whenever he could.

Nodding more to himself than to Sam, Rusty folded the photograph and slipped that into his pocket, too. "You got it."

"Call me if you come across anyone who thinks they might have seen anything unusual. Maybe someone actually saw her in a passing car." Sam knew it was a long shot, but as with lottery tickets, *someone* had to win—eventually.

Rusty nodded again, eager to get started. He stopped only long enough to look at the woman in the room with Sam. Even though the child's face was partially obscured by the baseball cap, he could see the resemblance between them. He'd always been good about details, picking up things others missed in passing.

"Don't worry," he said to her. "Sam'll find her. Sam's the best."

"How can you tell it's a girl?" Sam wanted to know. Between the jacket, cap and jeans, there was no hint of gender.

To Rusty, there was something definitely feminine about the set of the small face in the photograph, even partially obscured by a cap.

"I can always tell," Rusty assured him as he was leaving.

Sam nodded toward the computer. "Why don't you sign off now?" he said to Savannah.

He'd had her scan the latest image into the computer and post it on the web site. They'd gone as far as they could, filling in all the pertinent information as the blanks came up on the screen.

Savannah hit the appropriate keys on the keyboard and waited until the computer shut down. She turned off the monitor.

"What's next?" she wanted to know.

Though it was getting late in the day, they hadn't

stopped to eat since breakfast. He could do with some food, as could she, he thought.

"Next we try to force-feed you something. I know I could really go for a thick roast beef sandwich right about now." Sam stopped as he heard the office front door open and close again. He wasn't expecting anyone, and neither Megan nor Cade were due in for quite some time. He hoped it wasn't a new client. There was no one available to work another case.

Before Sam could step out into the reception area to see who it was, Rusty walked into the office. His helmet was hanging off his arm by the chin strap, and he was carefully carrying a large cardboard box.

"What's this?" Sam nodded at the box.

"You tell me. I found it in the hall just outside your front door." But instead of handing the box to Sam, he placed it on the desk in front of Savannah. Though Sam hadn't introduced them, when Rusty saw the name on the box, things clicked into place. He realized that he'd recognized her from the news broadcast he'd seen. "It's addressed to you."

She looked at Rusty blankly. "To me?"

"Care of the agency." Rusty was careful not to touch any more of the box than he already had. He pointed to the label as he glanced at Sam. "I guess they figured you'd bring it to her."

Savannah looked at the box uneasily. There were no stamps on it, canceled or otherwise, which meant the box had been hand-delivered by someone.

The kidnapper?

Eagerness to find out what was inside vied with

fear at what she might actually find. "Why didn't they just leave it on my doorstep?"

Everything kept pointing toward his theory, Sam thought. "My guess is that whoever left it wanted you to get this right away, but they didn't want to take a chance on being recognized. Maybe they thought someone would notice them dropping it off at your house." There was always a neighbor somewhere, looking out a window. "Someone who might know who they were."

Which meant that whoever had dropped off the box was someone who had been at, or at least reasonably near, her home before.

One theory might suggest a stalker, but he dismissed it quickly based on what Savannah had already told him. She'd received no messages, gotten no mysterious phone calls, no unwanted gifts—all typical calling cards for a stalker.

This was a kidnapper, not a stalker.

Taking a letter opener out of his desk, Sam turned the package toward him and began to work the opener under the tape running across the top.

But Savannah placed her hand over the handle, stopping him. He looked at her quizzically.

"It's addressed to me. I'll open it." Maybe it was silly, but it was important to her. Whatever was in this box had some sort of connection to Aimee. She wanted to be the one who opened it. "It's not as if we're dealing with a terrorist." Although he had struck terror into her heart by his heinous action. "At least, not one who leaves bombs."

Sam surrendered the letter opener to her. "Be my guest."

Savannah took the hilt in her hand and held her breath as she began working through the tape. What could the kidnapper have sent to her? If it *was* the kidnapper, she amended.

Maybe this was just some elaborate hoax by someone with a really sick sense of humor—and no heart.

She debated the point back and forth as she struggled with the tape. Savannah could feel her own heart beating hard.

It felt like an eternity before she finally cut through the tape and drew back the top of the box. Looking inside, a strangled gasp escaped her mouth.

"Oh, my God."

Blinking back tears, she pulled out a small article of clothing, and pressed it to her chest. It was a hooded pink sweatshirt with a frayed drawstring. Savannah could swear it still smelled faintly of her daughter.

She looked up at him. "It's Aimee's."

At first glance, the sweatshirt looked like a hundred other sweatshirts. There was nothing remarkable about it.

"Are you sure?" Sam pressed.

"I'm positive. One of the ties was frayed." She held it up. "See?" And then she turned large, luminous eyes up to Sam, pleading for him to make sense of this for her. "Why would the kidnapper send this to me?"

Sam took the sweatshirt from her and carefully examined it. It struck him that Aimee was small for her age. He turned it inside out slowly. There were no tears in the material, no pulled threads.

And most important, there was no sign of blood on the garment.

"My guess is that whoever sent it wanted you to know she was all right. Somehow, they thought this might be the proof you needed." Which made the kidnapper appear remarkably compassionate. The thought nagged at Sam. "There're no missing buttons, no rips. The sweatshirt's in good condition, ergo, so is the person who was wearing it."

It wasn't a conclusion Savannah would have reached on her own, but she took heart in his words.

Sam checked the pockets out of habit, though he didn't expect to find anything.

He was wrong.

There was a small folded piece of paper in the left pocket. Unfolding it, Sam saw the words in the middle of the page. It had come from a printer, an ink-jet one, judging by the smudge.

He read the words aloud to Savannah. "'She's all right.'"

"Let me see that." Savannah took it from him, wanting to read the words for herself. She stared at them. Was it true, or was whoever had taken Aimee just toying with her for some cruel reason of his own? "Just like the telephone message," she murmured. "The one the police couldn't trace."

The urge to take Savannah into his arms and comfort her was so strong that it held Sam in check for a moment. Overcoming it, he took the message from her and placed the paper back in the pocket. The entire package was going to the police lab for analysis.

Maybe this was the break they needed. "Someone's gone to a lot of trouble to set your mind at ease about Aimee," he said to Savannah.

"A considerate kidnapper." Rusty rolled the thought over in his mind. "Isn't that some kind of contradiction in terms?"

It was, from where Sam was standing.

"It's an oxymoron," he agreed.

He looked at Savannah. She'd taken the sweatshirt out of the box again and was hugging it to her, as if by holding it, she was somehow holding Aimee again. Sam could feel his heart twisting in pain for her.

"Savannah, we need to give that to Underwood." Gently, he coaxed the sweatshirt from her hands.

"I know." Her eyes were brighter when she raised them to look at him. Aimee was alive—that was all that mattered. That, and getting her back. "Elliott was right," she realized suddenly.

"Yes, he was."

For now—because Savannah had gotten the front seat on the roller coaster and just plunged down a steep incline before being dragged back up again—Sam let it alone. But there was something that didn't sit right with him about the other man. Maybe a part of him didn't like the closeness that appeared to exist between Savannah and Elliott. He didn't know. He did know that he had no right to that feeling.

It lingered just the same.

Rusty stood waiting. "Still want me to canvas the area?"

"More than ever." Sam closed the box carefully. Ready, he looked at Savannah, knowing there was no way that he could talk her into staying here until he got back. "Let's go back to see Underwood."

Ben Underwood dropped into a chair within the room he'd commandeered for his task force. He was exhausted and needed a quick break before meeting with the others to discuss further strategy.

Just five minutes, that's all he wanted. Five quiet minutes to himself.

He needed more than ten times that, but he would settle for what he could get. In the last seven weeks, as summer came to the sunny coastal city, there had been what seemed a rash of abductions to shake them up.

Closing his eyes, Ben rocked back in the chair. It squeaked a protest, which he ignored. He couldn't clearly remember when he'd slept last. Probably in another lifetime.

About as long as it'd been since he'd slept beside a warm body. His wife had long since left him—his own personal casualty in the city's ongoing war against crime. Ben sighed.

It irritated him beyond words that he didn't have nearly as many men working these cases as he would have wanted.

Not enough men, not enough time. By all rights, it should have been a slogan written across each police blotter so the new recruits coming in would know exactly what they were up against.

They'd all learn in time.

It vaguely occurred to Ben that he was making noises just like Sam Walters had just before Sam had left the force. At the time, he'd thought that Sam was a fool to throw away his career so soon after earning his detective's shield.

Now he wasn't all that sure.

Opening his eyes, Ben took out his own shield. He cradled it in the palm of his hand and studied it thoughtfully.

He'd traded his life for a piece of tin—a piece of tin and all the things it represented. But once in a while, he actually solved a case, actually made someone feel safe. Actually foiled a crime before it had a deadly consequence.

Maybe it wasn't such a bad trade after all.

A noise at the door caught his attention. Quickly pocketing his shield, Ben turned his chair to look toward the doorway. It surprised him to see that Sam was back.

Rousing himself, Ben got to his feet. "You again? You don't stop hanging around here, people'll start talking about us being an item."

The quirky smile faded from Ben's face when he realized that Sam was carrying a large brown box and that Savannah had come in behind him. He couldn't read her expression.

Because it was in his nature, he braced himself for the worst.

* * *

Aside from letting Underwood know about this latest development, the more Savannah thought about it, the more she saw no reason for giving him the sweatshirt. She wanted to hold on to it. Having it kept Aimee alive for her.

But she kept her questions to herself until after she and Sam were back in the parking lot in front of the police station. Underwood apparently didn't like having his methods questioned. He seemed like a dedicated enough police detective, but it was clear that he viewed her as an intruder, and, as such, he wasn't about to share anything with her.

That was for Sam to do.

"What good is sending Aimee's sweatshirt to the lab?" she wanted to know. "You can't get a decent set of prints off an article of clothing, can you?"

Taking her elbow, Sam ushered her toward his car. "Not usually, no, but there are other things they can find. Like samples of hair embedded in the weave, traces of things that might be in the area where they're holding her. A trace of systemic insecticide she might have brushed against before the sweatshirt was taken from her, for instance, might mean she's in or near a nursery of some sort. You'd be surprised what they can piece together in those labs."

"So there *is* hope." It was so slippery a thing, constantly sliding through her fingers. She needed to hear Sam reassure her. She was becoming increasingly dependent on his support. And him.

Chapter 11

Sam looked at her pointedly over the hood of the car. "There is *always* hope." He got in, and after a beat, she followed suit.

He waited until she buckled up before starting the car.

Savannah felt tired and wired at the same time. They'd put in a long day, but like the situation she found herself in, there seemed to be no end in sight. She turned her head toward Sam. "So where do we go from here?"

"Right now, we go get something to eat." He began to back out of the space. From the corner of his eye, he could see a protest forming on her lips. "I don't know about you, but I'm starved."

Before he could finish backing out, his cell phone rang. He put his foot on the brake.

It seemed to Savannah that everything else stopped as well. The car, the air. Time. There could be a million reasons why his phone rang, a million people calling him. She could only focus on one.

She held her breath, waiting.

Sam had flipped the phone open and was holding it against his ear. "This is Sam."

"Sam, I've got to knock off for now." Rusty's voice filled his ear. "But I can get started again early tomorrow morning. I don't have classes until one."

Sam glanced at the clock on the dashboard. Rusty had been at it approximately two hours. That wasn't much time. "How many houses did you get to?"

Rusty paused to gauge. "About a third, I'd guess. I wrote all the addresses down."

"Nothing?" Sam knew the answer before he asked, but there was always a chance that Rusty was saving this to be dramatic.

When he heard Rusty sigh, Sam knew the chance had faded away. "Nothing."

"All right. I'll talk to you tomorrow." Sam flipped the phone shut. Throughout the exchange, he'd felt Savannah's eyes on him. "That was Rusty, he's got—"

"Nothing, yes, I heard." She took a deep breath as if she were bracing herself for another plunge down on the roller coaster. As soon as he finished backing out of the parking space, she turned to face him. "Be honest with me, Sam. What are the chances of finding her?" Savannah couldn't bring herself to add the word *alive*.

But it haunted her.

Sam knew he could be brutally blunt and quote statistics, but what good would that do her? Besides, it wasn't his way. For one thing, statistics didn't take miracles into account. And he was a very firm believer in miracles. He had to be. The job wouldn't have been bearable if he wasn't.

Sam was careful to weave enthusiasm into his voice. "Still very good." He took the car onto the road. From here, the drive could be either quaint or scenic. With her in mind, he chose quaint. She needed distractions. "What do you feel like?"

That was easy. "As if everywhere I turn, there's ground glass."

He hurt for her, and that wasn't a good sign. It meant his objectivity was still slipping through his fingers, no matter how hard he tried to hold on to it. He was going to have to try harder.

Sam shook his head. "No, I mean what do you feel like having to eat?"

Her mouth felt like disembodied cardboard. The slight growl coming from her stomach might as well have belonged to someone else, for all the impression it made on her.

Savannah lifted one shoulder in a vague shrug. The last thing on her mind was food. "I don't care. Surprise me."

He thought of driving over to his favorite restaurant. It wasn't far from here. Built to resemble a little grass hut, its best tables faced the ocean. But it didn't take a detective to figure out that Savannah wasn't up to sitting in a restaurant, exchanging small talk while she waited for a dinner that she didn't want.

That left the ever-popular alternative. "How about takeout?"

The same uninterested shrug met his suggestion. "Sounds good."

He stopped by a place he frequented where the portions were a decent size and the prices left something in your pockets for another time. He figured there had to be something here she liked. If not, he did. One way or another, the food wouldn't go to waste.

Armed with a teeming large white bag with a red dragon breathing even redder fire embossed on the side, he returned to the car and drove Savannah to her house.

She hardly seemed aware of the trip.

He was worried about her.

Moving back and forth from the cupboard to the counter, Savannah put out several bowls and a handful of napkins. They'd gotten Chinese food. Because she'd left the choice entirely up to him, Savannah noticed he'd bought an assortment of entrees.

Unpacking the cartons, Sam looked at the napkins that she placed beside the bowls. "Expecting me to be sloppy?"

"I like to be prepared."

He didn't doubt it. He'd already gathered that Savannah King liked being in control of things, liked to be able to at least predict, if not actually call, the shots. Being in this sort of situation—both ends of the tunnel blocked off and no light coming in from any-where—had to be torture for her.

He crumpled up the bag to throw away, and saw her reaching for the silverware. "No, leave them."

"How are we supposed to eat this?" she asked.

"Why don't you try using chopsticks?" On a whim, he'd picked up two sets at the restaurant. Hold-ing them up now, he offered her a pair. She made no attempt to take them from him. "Have you ever eaten with them before?"

"No." She eyed the long white sticks, and picked up a few more napkins. This was going to get messy. "All right," she said gamely. "I'll try them. I'm not really hungry anyway."

He laughed at her expression. "It's easier than you think."

Sitting down, she pulled a carton of sweet-and-sour pork to her and emptied some into a bowl. "It would have to be."

She picked up the chopsticks and tried to eat, but it was like trying to coordinate small knitting needles with a mind of their own. More than half a dozen tries later, every bit of food that she picked up still rained down to the bowl before it reached her lips.

With a sigh, she put the chopsticks down.

Sam had little success in hiding his amusement. "Looking at you, I would have thought you'd have much better hand-eye coordination."

Savannah frowned at the offending utensils. "I do, when I'm not trying to eat with narrow knitting nee-dles."

"It's all in the fingers," he coached, holding up his own pair. Hungry, he'd made short work of his servings.

She raised an eyebrow at the statement. "And how many years in detective school did it take for you to come up with that?"

So, she still had a sense of humor. It was an encouraging sign.

"Wise guy." Putting the chopsticks down, Sam picked them up again for her benefit, showing her just where to place her fingers. "You hold them like this."

Attempts to mimic him failed. With a laugh, she surrendered and retired her chopsticks to the counter. "This is definitely not good for my self-esteem."

"Can't have that." Sliding off his stool, Sam came around behind her. "Here, you do it like this." He covered her fingers with his own and guided her through the steps in slow motion. "You pick up some rice—"

"And then you drop it," she said, watching the grains fall.

"No, then you eat it. Try again." This time, he was successful in getting a small bit of chicken to her mouth. His breath caught as he watched it slip between her lips. Heat came from nowhere, enveloping him like a quick blast from a suddenly opened furnace. Sam's eyes met hers.

Something tightened in his gut.

He'd always put a lot of stock in intuition. And his was telling him to back away.

This time, he didn't listen.

"And we have liftoff," he pronounced in a voice that was barely above a whisper.

The smile on Savannah's lips melted slowly as triumph gave way to feelings that had nothing to do with mastering chopsticks.

Without a word, Savannah placed the chopsticks on the table and turned her stool so that she was directly facing him.

Sam was afraid to take the first step.

Afraid not to.

He knew that once he did, there would be no road to lead him back. No bridge to shimmy across on his belly and deny that any of this had ever happened.

There would be only forward. And forward was a place without parameters, without borders. An unknown place.

It was best to stay clear.

But forward beckoned to him with a fierce pull that he found impossible to resist.

And so he didn't.

Sam took Savannah into his arms and kissed her. The tangy taste that seeped into his consciousness had nothing to do with the small, opened cartons that stood littering her kitchen counter. It was something that he knew belonged to her alone. A way to brand her in his mind.

If his mind was ever operational again.

A tangle of emotions swept through him—emotions he was not up to dealing with. Emotions he didn't think he'd ever have to deal with again. Desire, passion, urges—all the things he'd kept so well under wraps were now trying to burst free.

Were bursting free.

It was as if every semblance of control was being ripped out of his hands, and there wasn't a damn thing he could do about it.

But if he couldn't, she'd have to. Drawing back, Sam looked at her. "You're making it very hard to remember all the rules."

She liked that. Jarred had given her flowery words to make her head spin. Sam was giving her something better. He was giving her his honesty. Somewhere in the recesses of that part of her heart that still beat, that still clung to hope, she'd always known that would be her undoing.

An honest man.

"Just for tonight—" she raised her eyes to his "—couldn't you forget that there are rules?"

That was just the trouble. He was already forgetting. Forgetting everything except the way she heated his blood, the way she made him want to make love to every inch of her.

The way she looked at him took his very breath away. He pressed a kiss to her throat, to the outline of her ear, to her neck. When she twisted against him, a soft, surrendering moan escaping her lips, Sam felt his pulse jump.

"Are you sure?" he whispered into her hair, praying that she'd answer "yes." If she drew away from him now, at this last possible moment, he wasn't sure that he could stand it.

That's what they have cold showers for. The thought echoed through his brain, mocking him.

There wasn't enough cold water in the world.

But Savannah didn't draw away. Instead, she turned her face up to his again, her answer in her eyes. Very slowly, he ran his hands along her body, caressing her. Memorizing her.

He hadn't realized just how beautiful she was—and how very much he wanted her—until this minute.

"I'm sure," she whispered. The words feathered along his skin, tantalizing him. Breaking the very last strand of control he had left to reel himself in.

This couldn't go anywhere, he told himself. Wouldn't go anywhere. He couldn't do this...

Without another word, her breath warming his skin, he brought his mouth down to hers.

One kiss flowered into another and then another, each with a little more passion, a little more eagerness, than the last. His pulse began to accelerate, the rhythm soon rivaling the engine of a jet.

The depth of his desire surprised him.

The magnitude of her response surprised him more.

With each kiss, Savannah became more pliant, more giving. More hungry. As he molded her to him, she sealed herself against him, her arms twisting about his neck, her mouth questing his.

It was a dance, just inches short of a competition. For every step he took, every movement he made, she matched him and did one better. Exciting him. Exciting herself.

It was as if, for this one magic night, two kindred

souls had somehow managed to find one another in a world full of lost souls.

He couldn't get enough of her. Couldn't touch her enough, kiss her enough, breath in her scent enough. It was as if he'd taken leave of any senses he'd ever professed to have.

And he didn't care. All that mattered was making love with her. Pleasuring her.

Maybe this was crazy, Savannah thought, but at this moment she desperately needed crazy. Needed to have her mind swirl and her feelings churn. Needed not to think at all, but only to feel. To stop taking one step after another and finally feel the ground beneath her feet, the sky above her head. If only for one moment, one hour. One night.

The wondrous magic of his mouth propelled her to a place where there was no pain, no horrors, and where the only sensation was a deep, pervading pleasure that consumed her inch by melting inch until it owned her completely.

He was a thoughtful lover, a gentle lover. A passionate lover. Sam was all things at once, each new turn a surprise, and she strove to keep up with him. He made her discover things about herself that she had never even suspected existed.

She had no idea that pleasure went so deep or desire so far.

Or that she was capable of giving that pleasure back. But the moan that throbbed in his throat and echoed in her head bore witness to the fact. The thought excited her even more.

She felt his hands on her body, at first reverently, then eagerly, unbuttoning her blouse, unzipping her skirt. Slipping away her undergarments.

Setting her free.

There was no awkwardness to meet the movements, no momentary flash of embarrassment the way there had been with Jarred. She instinctively knew that Sam wasn't judging her, wasn't comparing her to others he'd had.

By his very touch, he made her feel special. Made her feel safe. And she would always be grateful to him for that.

Her gratitude spilled out and mixed with all the other emotions and sensations dancing through her.

She met him step for step. As his hands moved over her, slowly drawing away her clothing, she shadowed his movements, taking off his shirt, his trousers, the dark blue briefs that clung to his torso, testifying to his desire for her.

As the last shred of clothing between them fell to the floor, Sam dived his fingers into her hair, framing her face with his palms. For a moment, he just looked at her and knew that he was on the most dangerous ground he'd ever tread. There was quicksand just beneath his feet, and if he wasn't careful, he'd disappear completely without a trace.

He threw caution to the wind.

Over and over again his mouth slanted over hers until they were both reduced to pure blue flames that burned desperately for one another.

It had been long—so very long—since she'd made

love with a man. If he didn't take her soon, she thought she would explode. He'd touched, caressed, stroked and suckled until every fiber of her being was ripe for the taking. For the joining.

Suddenly, with his mouth sealed to hers again, she felt herself being lifted into his arms. Confused, lungs bursting for air, she moved her head back to look at him.

"You don't want it to be on the kitchen floor."

He was being thoughtful of her, even now. Savannah wrapped her arms around his neck, bringing her mouth back to his. "I don't care. I just want it to be with you."

It was his final undoing.

He groaned again as he kissed her, knowing he'd used up the last reserve he had. Restraint was no longer possible.

They made it as far as the living room. There, on the sofa, Sam made love with Savannah as if there would be no tomorrow. No reckoning. No consequences to face.

He made love to her as if he'd been waiting for her all of his life. And, at that moment, he could have sworn that he had been.

Because making love with her, having her body move urgently as he finally sheathed himself within her, as he felt her tighten around him, made him feel more alive than he ever remembered feeling.

As the final sensation burst, squeezing the last bit of energy from Savannah before letting her fall back, exhausted on the sofa, she felt a quickening in her heart.

She remained very still as the sensation grew and then drenched her.

The wise thing would be to ignore it, or if it couldn't be ignored, to deny it. Deny it with the last breath she had. She'd been this route before, felt this way before, and it had all turned to dust.

But denial was futile. Whatever came afterward wouldn't change what she felt right at this moment. Perhaps even for all the moments to come. He was the kindest and most exciting man she'd ever known.

And she was in love with him.

It was something, she resolved, that he was never going to know.

The heat refused to leave his body even after his senses returned, scrambling across him like so many unwanted house guests. He'd had her, and the desire hadn't left. If anything, it had only intensified.

But he could think now, whereas he couldn't before. Think and upbraid and be ashamed of himself, of what he'd allowed himself to do.

He drew away from her—only inches away, but she could feel the change in him instantly. He might as well have been miles away.

"I'm sorry."

The words slashed at her like a cold steel blade aimed at her heart, but she refused to bleed. Instead, she asked, "Why?"

He didn't know where to begin, how to make amends. Sorry wasn't good enough, yet he had nothing else. "Because I took advantage of you. Because I couldn't—"

She'd heard about as much as she could take. Without thinking, she smacked the palm of her hand against his back. "Why, you pompous bastard."

Stunned, Sam could only turn around and stare at her. "Excuse me?"

"Do you think that little of me?"

It was himself he thought little of, not her. "No, I just said—"

"What you said makes me out to be some addle-brained woman who can be led around by the nose." Ignoring the fact that she was still nude, Savannah rose to her knees, fire in her eyes. "You didn't take advantage of me—or the situation, if that's your next guess. If I didn't want this to happen—if I didn't want you—then we wouldn't be here like this. I'd be in my room and you'd be out here. Alone."

Speechlessness dissipated, dissolving into a wide grin that encompassed all his features. God, but he wanted her again. "Has anyone ever told you you're magnificent when you're angry?"

"Flattery isn't going to get you anywhere." But her anger was already slipping away from her, rendered hazy by the light in his eyes.

The expression on his face was positively wicked. "What is?"

Savannah pretended to think. "You could try kissing me again."

Lying down again, Sam pulled her to him until she was directly over him, the ends of her hair tickling his chest. Teasing him. ''You know, I just might do that.''

''Well?'' There was a smile in her eyes. ''You talk too much.''

''So I've been told.'' Cupping the back of her head, Sam brought her mouth down to his.

Chapter 12

"If you're thinking of going off without me, you're in for a rude awakening."

Sam almost nicked himself. Only sharply honed reflexes made him freeze quickly enough to avoid digging the edge of the razor into his flesh. His eyes met Savannah's in the bathroom mirror. He'd left her sleeping, but here she was standing behind him.

"The thought did cross my mind."

Carefully, he slid the razor down his cheek, scraping away stubble and soap. He'd hunted through the medicine cabinet and under the sink, but hadn't been able to find shaving cream anywhere. He felt the stubble resisting and pinching. Sam had half a mind to leave the one-day growth.

Rinsing off the razor, Sam tried to explain his reasoning for thinking that she was better off staying at home. "This has to be getting frustrating for you."

"Not as frustrating as sitting around, doing nothing is." Her navy-blue towel was anchored around his otherwise nude torso, and there were random beads of water still clinging to his body. Feelings of intimacy permeated her from all sides. Savannah wasn't quite sure how to deal with them.

He realized he'd taken something of hers without asking. Pausing before taking another pass at his face, Sam held up the razor.

"I borrowed this. I hope you don't mind. But it was either that, or go back to my place."

He studied her over his shoulder. The scent of sleep and lovemaking clung to her skin like an enticing perfume. The last remnants of sleep still shadowed her eyes. It took him a moment to focus his thoughts. It took him longer to talk himself out of wanting her all over again.

"I didn't want to waste the time," he added, the words slowly leaving his lips. He forced himself to look back at his own image in the mirror.

"I appreciate that. Feel free to use whatever you need." Savannah dragged wisps of tousled blond hair out of her eyes. "Give me ten minutes, I'll be ready," she promised.

The next moment, she'd disappeared into the bedroom again.

Ten minutes? Who was she kidding? "No woman can get ready in ten minutes." Hell, even he couldn't get ready that fast.

Her voice drifted back to him out of the depths of her closet. "I can."

She could, and did.

He'd come downstairs to the kitchen to find that Savannah was already there ahead of him. Surprised, he stood in the doorway and shook his head. "You're a woman of hidden talents."

The most surprising of which, he had to admit, had come out last night. He wouldn't have guessed, despite the initial attraction he'd felt, that there was such passion so close to the surface.

Maybe he wasn't as good a detective as he'd like to think, he mused.

Sam moved around the kitchen with the ease of a man who could make himself at home anywhere. Opening the refrigerator, he took out several cartons of the leftover Chinese food and lined them up beside the microwave.

"How do you feel about leftovers for breakfast?" Anticipating her response, he glanced in her direction. "You get to use a fork this time if you like." There was a smile in his eyes. "If we go the chopsticks route again, I'm afraid we might never get out of the house."

Popping the cartons onto the microwave turntable, he closed the door and set the timer.

She'd come down anticipating the smell of food that was turning bad. The last she remembered, they'd left all the cartons out on the counter. The counter she looked at was empty, and clean.

"When did you put all the cartons into the refrigerator?"

He took the plates that had been draining in the sink. "I also washed the dishes." He indicated the plates he was holding.

She frowned, trying to remember. They'd made love into the wee hours of the night. "When?"

"Last night. Closer to this morning, I guess." His thoughts had kept him up. Not all of them had centered on his case. Too many, in fact, had focused on her. "You sleep pretty soundly."

She thought of the nights that had come before, where nightmares had given her little peace. "Only when I'm completely exhausted."

Sam took out a fork for her; he chose chopsticks for himself. "I take that as a compliment."

She only smiled.

It was while he'd been puttering around in the kitchen that he'd made up his mind to reestablish the barriers between them. It was the only way.

That had been the plan he'd decided on, and it was a good plan, a sound plan. A workable plan.

Until he'd looked at her this morning. And wanted her all over again.

She was going to regret last night; he was certain of it. Once she regained perspective, once she and Aimee were reunited and Savannah realized that she'd mistaken her feelings of gratitude for something far stronger, she was going to regret making love with him.

The thought moved through him like a funeral dirge. He tried not to think about that, too.

The list of things he couldn't think about was growing.

The microwave timer went off. Opening the door, Savannah made her choice.

A carton of fried rice in her hand, she sat down on the stool beside him. There was no disputing the fact that she was eager to get started. But part of her wanted to linger, just for a tiny moment, with this man who had happened into her life after she'd given up all thoughts of ever feeling anything for anyone again.

Was that so wrong, to try to mine happiness where she found it, even under adverse circumstances?

Savannah had no answer for that.

Focusing on Aimee, she asked, "Are we going to canvas those houses along with Rusty?"

"I'm thinking of playing something a little closer to home," Sam said as he mixed what was left in the three cartons together.

It sounded mysterious, and she wondered if he was phrasing it that way because he anticipated a resistance to his suggestion. But any wariness she'd felt before had abruptly faded. Something magical had happened to her while they'd made love last night. Savannah believed in him now. Believed that Sam would do everything in his power to find Aimee.

It wasn't just a matter of earning his money; this was something he was honor-bound to do. She knew that, felt that. And waited to hear what he had to say.

"And that is?"

Sam approached the subject carefully. He knew how she'd reacted to this earlier, and he didn't want to upset her. But it had to be faced.

"I keep coming back to the phone call and the note." He set the carton down and looked at her. "When Elliott called you that last time, he had you on speakerphone. How many people were around, do you think, when you said you wished there was some way you could be assured that Aimee was all right?"

Closing her eyes, she tried to summon back the moment—the voices she'd been able to distinguish. "There was Elliott, Larry, Vera." Then, opening her eyes, she shook her head. "A few others, maybe. It's hard to say."

He nodded. "That's okay." He intended to go through all of them anyway. "Did you have to be fingerprinted when you came to work for Big Bytes?"

She thought it an odd question. "No, we design computer software for games predominantly. We don't handle any kind of sensitive government material." That would be the only situation she could think of to require fingerprinting. That, or an arrest. "What are you getting at?"

If the lab found any fingerprints on the box, beyond hers and Rusty's, it still wouldn't mean anything unless they had something to compare them to, Sam thought.

"Maybe nothing."

His cell phone, perched on the recharger where

he'd set it up last night, rang, temporarily tabling the conversation.

As soon as the sound shattered the air, Savannah could feel every nerve ending within her body coming to attention. Waiting.

Sam opened the cell phone. "Hello, this is Sam."

"Sam, it's Rusty. I think you might want to come down here and talk to this guy I spoke to this morning. He thinks he might have seen someone driving off in a car with Aimee in it. At least," Rusty amended, "he said he saw a little kid who looked like the one in the photograph struggling with somebody in a car. The car was going south on MacArthur Boulevard, right by the mall."

That was good enough for Sam. "Where are you?"

Sam urgently gestured toward Savannah for something to write with. Finding a pen, she grabbed the first writing surface she came across, and shoved both at him. Sam wound up scribbling the address Rusty gave him on the inside of a butterfly-design paper napkin.

"Got it." Sam reread the address to himself just to make sure he could. "We'll be there as soon as we can. Stay put."

Savannah waited only long enough for Sam to flip the phone closed. "Well?"

"Don't get your hopes up," he warned, knowing she would anyway. "But Rusty thinks he found someone who might have seen the kidnapper drive off with Aimee."

Thinks. Might. Ever since they'd started looking for

her daughter, every path they'd turned to had been littered with vague words.

But vague words were all she had, so she clung to them tightly. And hoped.

"Let's go!" Slinging her purse over her shoulder, Savannah hurried to the front door.

Still holding the cell phone, Sam grabbed an egg roll and followed her out. He had no idea when his next meal would be.

Harvey Silverstone was retired and lonely. A people-person of long standing, he was more than happy to relate his story for the three people sitting in his airless living room, embellishing it as he went along to hold his audience for as long as possible.

It took tact and precision for Sam to get him to hurry his narrative along before it expanded to the proportions of an epic poem.

Looking just a little deflated, Mr. Silverstone curtailed the details of his discussion with his wife prior to his venturing out with his bullmastiff for their midmorning walk around the perimeter of the Primrose Development. With much prodding, he got to the heart of the matter.

"I was walking along with Kong when he stopped to answer the call of nature." He winked slyly at Savannah. "It takes him a while these days. Not like in the old days, but then, we're both getting on a bit."

"Mr. Silverstone," Sam prodded.

"Right. Anyway. I'm waiting on him, looking at the traffic, when I see this car pass by. Dark-blue

Honda. Accord. 'Ninety-five model.'' He smiled broadly. "Used to sell cars for a living. There isn't a vehicle out there that I can't pinpoint the year on.''

Well, that was fortunate at least, Sam thought. Maybe they were finally getting a break. "Did you see anything that made you suspicious?''

"That's what I told this boy here.'' He nodded at Rusty. "The driver went right through a red light. Lucky for him, there wasn't one of Newport's finest around. Would've slapped him with a two-hundred-dollar ticket for sure.''

Savannah felt as if she wanted to run down the man's throat and pull out the pertinent words. "You said something about a child?''

"That's probably why he went through the light. There was a little kid on the passenger side. From where I was standing, it looked like the kid was trying to roll down the window. He was yanking the kid back into the seat and not paying attention to the road. Don't know how they got across without somebody running into them. Guess when it's not your time—''

Sam rose to his feet, and Rusty sprang up with him. Savannah was half a beat behind, anxious to follow up this lead.

Sam shook the man's hand. "Thank you for your help, Mr. Silverstone.''

"Sure thing.'' The man lumbered to his feet as well, looking crestfallen. "You don't all have to leave, do you?''

"I'm afraid so.'' Sam felt Savannah urgently tugging on his hand. "We're trying to track down the child you think you might have seen."

"No 'think' about it." Harvey followed them to the door. "I saw a kid, plain as day."

"We appreciate your help." Savannah was already outside the house, waiting for him to join her.

"Then I suppose you'd be wanting the license number as well."

Sam stopped dead and turned around. Why hadn't the man said anything before this? "You have the license number?"

"Sure do." Pleased as punch, Harvey rattled off the number. "It's a game I play to keep my mind sharp. I memorize everything. Hell—'scuse me, little lady," he apologized to Savannah. "As I was saying, I've gotten so that I can memorize whole columns in newspapers."

Uttering his thanks again, Sam hurried Savannah and Rusty out before Mr. Silverstone felt called upon to give them a full demonstration.

Rusty left them at the curb. "If you don't need me for anything else, I've got to stop at the library before I go to class."

"You did great," Sam told him. Rusty beamed, then hurried off to his motorcycle.

Now all they had to do was verify Silverstone's story, Sam thought.

Once in his car, Sam called on ahead to his office and asked Alex to track down a license plate number, name and address.

"Oh, God, Sam," Savannah murmured as he hung up. "This is too good to be true."

That was just what he was afraid of. When things seemed too good to be true, they generally were. But he didn't say as much to her.

"Hang on just a little longer, Savannah," Sam told her.

By the time they arrived at the office twenty minutes later, Alex was waiting with the name and address of the owner of the car.

"Don F. Starling," Sam read aloud, then looked at Savannah for any sign of recognition. "The name mean anything to you?"

Savannah shook her head. "Never heard it before."

Maybe his theory had been all wrong after all. Wouldn't be the first time.

Looking at the address, Sam got an itchy feeling through his shoulders. The one he always got when something didn't feel just right.

"Well, what are we waiting for?" Savannah wanted to know. "Let's go."

He caught her hand, wanting to talk to her before they left. Wanting to prepare her for the possible disappointment she might have to face.

"Savannah, this might turn out to be a wild-goose chase. Silverstone could have been mistaken about what he thought he saw, or maybe he got the license scrambled and it's not this car at all, or—"

"I know, I know." Savannah understood what he was trying to do, to cushion a possible fall. She appreciated that, but while they stood here talking, if it *was* the right man, he could be moving on—with her daughter. "But I still can't help hoping—"

"Yeah, me too." He opened the door for her.

Savannah hurried outside. Reaching the car first, she waited impatiently for him to unlock it. "Do we have to go to Underwood?" She assumed that was the next step, though she would rather just get to Starling directly.

"No, not yet. We need to do a little more checking first." This was different from bringing in Aimee's sweatshirt, or asking the police to drag a lake. This very possibly could be a dead end. He didn't want to waste Underwood's time if it was. It was something he could handle on his own, one way or another.

Nerves were pole-vaulting through Savannah's body by the time they parked several doors down from the Laguna Hills single-story house where Don Starling lived. Just before Sam got out, she placed her hand on his arm.

"Are you sure we shouldn't call in the police?"

He was sure. "We might be wrong." And they'd already put Ben through one wild-goose chase at the lake. If he struck out twice, there would be no getting to bat a third time.

She didn't want to be wrong. She wanted this to be over. To go home with Aimee in her arms. "And if we're right?"

He understood the unspoken question. "Then you follow my lead, and if anything looks wrong to you—

anything at all—'' he emphasized, ''I want you out of there. Fast.'' He would rather leave her in the car as a precaution while he went to the house, but he knew he hadn't a prayer of persuading her.

Sam pulled a gun from where it was tucked into the back of his jeans, and took off the safety. Savannah stared at the weapon.

''When did you—?''

''Just after you sailed out of the office. That's why I wasn't right behind you.''

Tucking it back into place and covering it with his jacket, he motioned her out of the car.

The pseudo-Cape Cod house looked innocuous enough as she approached it with Sam. Maybe that was what the kidnapper was counting on. Savannah braced herself, as Sam rang the doorbell.

He rang it several times before there was an answer. The sound of a little girl screaming from within the house had Savannah clutching Sam's hand.

''Is that her?'' he asked.

''I can't tell.'' What was wrong with her? she thought. A mother should be able to tell her own child's screams. Why wasn't she certain?

The door was opened by a tall, heavyset man. He looked clearly annoyed.

Glaring at them, he growled, ''Yeah?''

'''Scuse us for bothering you,'' Sam drawled in a heavy, Texas accent. ''But our car went dead. That's it down there.'' He pointed vaguely down the block. ''None of your neighbors are in. I was wondering if we could use your telephone to call a tow truck. My missus is feeling a little faint—what from the heat and all. It's a hot one today, isn't it?'' Sam felt that would explain Savannah's pale face.

The man looked at them skeptically, as if debating. Another scream came from within the house. Sam took the opportunity to elbow his way in past him. Surprise was his best weapon.

''Hey, what do you think you're doing?'' Starling demanded, more alarmed now than angry.

At that moment, a blond little girl came rushing into the room, still screeching at the top of her lungs. She was being chased by a little boy who looked to be a little younger than she was.

For an instant, while the girl was still a blur, Savannah's heart leaped into her throat. But even before she had a chance to focus on the girl's face, she knew it wasn't Aimee.

The girl abruptly stopped yelling and stared at the strangers with keen interest. The boy bumped into her, and she pushed him away. He began to cry.

''Who are they, Daddy?''

''That's what I want to know,'' the man said uneasily. ''If you're here to rob us, the only thing I've got worth anything is right here in this room.'' He placed a protective arm around each child.

''I'm sorry,'' Sam apologized. ''It looks like we've made a mistake.'' He went to take Savannah's arm, but she crossed to the little girl.

''How old is she?'' Savannah asked the man. The ache in her chest felt large enough to choke her.

Fear left the man's face, only to be replaced with suspicion. "What's this all about, anyway?"

"A misunderstanding." Sam shook his head. "Long story. Sorry to have bothered you."

The man studied Sam and Savannah for a moment. Finally, he said, "Gerrie's five." He sighed wearily. "It's like having triplets. I can never get her to sit still. Even in the car with a seat belt, she's all over everything. I'm going to have to wind up tying her up one of these days."

That would explain the struggle that Silverstone witnessed, Sam thought.

"Their mother's in the hospital right now," he told Savannah, "having another. I don't think I can take it."

"Yes," Savannah said softly, stroking the little girl's blond hair, "you can. Thank you for your help."

Sam slipped his arm around Savannah's shoulders as he ushered her out. Any promises he'd made to himself this morning about reestablishing boundaries had temporarily been put on hold. She needed comfort.

"How are you holding up?"

"I'm all right."

But he knew by the hollow tone in her voice that she was far from that.

Returning to his office, Sam knew they were back to square one. And to his original gut feeling. The kidnapper had tried to reassure Savannah. To Sam that meant that this was not a professional ring, out to steal children to fill a market quota. This was an amateur—someone who had taken Aimee out of some unknown desperation.

Someone who had feelings.

Someone, Sam felt fairly confident, who was rather well acquainted with Savannah's life.

Savannah paced the length of Sam's office. Though she trusted his instincts, what he said still went against everything she held dear. She didn't like it any more now than when he'd first suggested it.

"But why? Why would someone I know want to kidnap Aimee? What would their reason be?"

"If I knew that, I wouldn't have to try to figure out who it was. I'd know." He switched on his computer. A preliminary check through accessible records had yielded nothing. As far as the police were concerned, the people who worked at Big Bytes were clean. But there were other records that could be checked. "I need to get my hands on as much information as I can about the people who work with you." Someone in the office the day they had come in had Aimee— he was fairly certain of it. "Now you said there are no fingerprints on file, but there have to be some kind of records."

She nodded. "What are you looking for?"

"I don't know," he admitted. It was a matter of knowing it when he saw it. "If I did, we could find it a lot faster."

"The employee records are in a database." One that she had helped tailor to the company's needs at

Larry's request. "Marital status, age, education," she enumerated, "health history forms."

The last struck a chord. It was as good a place as any to start. "How about fertility testing?"

She sat down at his desk. "That would be in insurance records, although I'm not sure if our insurance covers it." His logic eluded her. What did fertility tests have to do with Aimee? "What are you thinking?"

"Maybe someone at work was trying to have a baby. The stress of trying and failing can take a toll on a marriage after a while. Make you desperate. Maybe make you act a little crazy."

The jump from point A to point B was extreme, she thought. "Enough to steal Aimee? Under those circumstances, wouldn't they have tried to steal a baby—not a four-year-old?"

"I'm reaching," he admitted. "But if we go through all the personnel records, we might find something. Maybe a couple put in for adoption and were turned down. If someone came to check them out, it would be noted in the file, wouldn't it?"

"Possibly." Savannah bit her lower lip. "I'm going to have to hack into the records."

Megan was the one who was a whiz at the keyboard. He'd been prepared to wait for her. He looked at her dubiously.

"Can you?"

"I redesigned the program." Of course, this would be working without it, but there were ways around that. "Give me a while."

A while might be all that they had. Sam shoved his hands into his pockets and waited, uncomfortable in the knowledge that this lead might not take them any-where, either. And then he would have failed Savan-nah on two counts. Because he hadn't found her daughter, and because he'd allowed his own feelings to get in the way of his better judgment and gotten involved with her emotionally. It shouldn't have hap-pened, but it was too late for regrets.

The only way he could make it up to her was to find Aimee—no matter what it took.

Chapter 13

Sam felt as if his eyes were crossing. Blinking, he massaged his temples, trying to alleviate the tension building there. A little of it dissipated. The rest remained, hovering, waiting to take over the moment he started working again.

They'd been at this for hours, he and Savannah, searching through a mountain of hay for something that might vaguely resemble a needle if held up to the light in just the right way.

All they kept finding was more hay.

Sam slumped in his chair and stared at the screen, no longer seeing the data. It was all beginning to run together for him. Six years of accumulated information on sixty-five people made for a great deal of reading. And he read everything, refusing to skip over the smallest detail—afraid that if he did, he would miss the one all-important lead.

So far, there was no lead, all-important or otherwise. Just one hell of a headache in the making.

It was time to stop.

Leaning back, Sam glanced through the open door that led into Megan's office. Savannah was sitting ramrod straight at Megan's desk, going over the same records. He figured that two sets of eyes were better than one, and she knew the people she was reading about. She'd know if something was off-kilter or unusual.

How could she sit so perfectly straight after all these hours? It made him tired just looking at her.

It made him ache, just looking at her.

And remember. Last night came vividly back to him. Guilt trailed after, but not even a close second. He was too tired for that.

But not too tired to want her.

With effort, Sam shook off the thought.

He reached for his hamburger, and remembered, when his fingers came in contact with only an empty, greasy wrapper, that he'd eaten it. Alex had gone down to the local drive-through two hours before to get a couple of orders of burgers and fries for Savannah and him.

Now that he thought of it, the fries were still sitting like a hard lump in the pit of his stomach. He was going to have to remember to take his business elsewhere. Either that, or stock up on antacids.

Alex, he knew, had gone home more than an hour ago. It was time to do the same.

Stretching, Sam pushed his foot against the desk leg and eased his chair back. There was no point in trying to read any more health claims tonight. They were all beginning to meld together for him. He scooped up the empty wrapper and crumpled French fries container and tossed them into the wastepaper basket, then rose to his feet.

Walking into Megan's office, he came up behind Savannah. Her eyes intent on the screen, she didn't seem to realize he was in the room. Her long blond hair was pushed over to one side, dipping down so that the ends brushed against her breast, the way he longed to.

What he needed, he told himself as he watched her, was a cold beer. And fewer warm thoughts. The former wasn't available. The latter came anyway.

Sam looked at her desk. The takeout sack that Alex had brought to her was still standing there, its contents leaving a deepening stain on the bottom. He should have known, Sam thought.

If her back was straight, her shoulders were as stiff as a pair of work gloves left out in the rain. That couldn't be good. Moving behind her, Sam placed his hands on her shoulders. He meant to knead out some of the tension there.

Surprised, Savannah jumped in her chair.

"Sorry, didn't mean to scare you. You look tense," he explained when she jerked around to look at him.

He left his hands where they were—gentling her

the way a wrangler would a skittish colt. Very slowly, he began to knead.

Savannah tried to relax. It felt impossible. There was too much going on inside her.

"I feel like a Peeping Tom." With a sign, she withdrew her fingers from the keyboard and dropped them in her lap. "I know these people. I shouldn't be doing this."

Her knowing them was exactly the point, but he refrained from mentioning it again. He turned Savannah's chair halfway around until she faced him. Holding on to the armrests, he leaned forward until his face was level with hers.

"Why don't we knock it off for tonight?" he suggested. "We've been at this for hours, and maybe we just need to be fresher."

She had a different idea. She dragged her hand restlessly through her hair. "Or maybe we're wasting our time and there's nothing here."

"Maybe," he allowed. There was always that very real possibility. "But right now, I don't have any better ideas. There's no one left to question outright. No one else has reported seeing her. The lab analysis of her sweatshirt isn't in yet." And even if it was, he knew he would have to drag it out of Ben. Covertly. "We've talked to all the people in and around the mall several times over with no new information. Checking out the people who called on the 800 number hasn't produced any leads, either." This he'd gotten by way of a friend of his who worked in Ben's office. "You've gone on the news—"

Savannah raised her hand defensively to stave off any more words.

"I know all that," she snapped, then flushed. "Sorry."

Sam nodded, knowing it was the stress and not Savannah talking. "It's okay."

She looked back at the screen. She was up to the *R*s. Elliott's medical chart was pulled up. Seeing it spread across the screen rubbed against her conscience. "But this just seems wrong somehow."

There was a time to listen to your conscience, and a time to ignore it. This was one of those gray areas that she was paying him for.

Crooking his finger beneath her chin, he drew her attention back to him. Sam's eyes held hers. "Is it wrong to find Aimee?"

"No, of course not—"

"And if this leads us to her..." Sam's voice trailed off meaningfully.

She turned to look at the screen again. Sam's hand brushed against her cheek, reminding her how safe she'd felt in his arms last night. Safe and protected and confident that everything would be resolved.

The feeling seemed a million miles away right now. Savannah desperately needed it back. "You really think it will?"

He thought of the sweatshirt. It had been sent to her because of what she'd said. He'd bet his soul on it. "Yes. Right now, it's the best bet we have."

Glancing at the grease-sodden paper bag, he picked

it up and tossed it into the wastepaper basket. Then, taking her hand, Sam urged Savannah to her feet.

"C'mon, I'll buy you something better on the way home."

She nodded. "All right."

Pushing the chair back in, Sam leaned over Megan's desk to shut off the computer. He recognized the last name across the top of the screen. Savannah had been looking at Elliott's records. Going through them was probably what had triggered her reaction. He stared at it now, his hand hovering over the sequence of keys to shut down the machine.

Something about the file had bothered him when he'd pulled it up himself half an hour ago. Something that teased the back of his mind, flittering in and out like an elusive title to an old song he only half remembered. The harder he tried, the less it came to him. He'd gone on with his search, his feelings unresolved.

The reproduced copy of the claim form was no different on her monitor than it had been on his. Nothing came to him.

And yet—yet there was something....

Sam sighed. It was probably nothing more than frustration on his part. The man had a wife and daughter, and from what he'd read in the file, looked to be stability personified. There was nothing unusual, nothing outstanding, except—if Savannah's impression was correct—the man was a little henpecked. Elliott Reynolds had enough to deal with, without someone delving into his life with a magnifying glass.

Besides, there was no earthly reason for Elliott to kidnap Aimee. He had a daughter of his own.

Pressing the keys, Sam waited until the screen went black. Then he shut off the monitor.

He turned and saw Savannah standing there, looking fragile for all her capability and bravado. Seeing her like that made up his mind for him. Tomorrow he'd get back to all his fine resolutions and make them work. Tonight, Savannah looked as if she needed a shoulder—if not to cry on, then at least to lean on. And his were broad.

He slipped his arm around her shoulders, and they walked out.

Savannah put down her napkin. Tonight they'd brought home a pizza, and she had actually eaten two slices. The aroma made it impossible not to.

Just like being around Sam made it impossible not to hope.

She blessed the whim of fate that had brought to her the article she'd read about their agency. To the article, and Sam.

For a second she sat there, studying him as he finished what she'd counted was his fifth slice. She decided the man had to be hollow; from what she'd seen, he ate well and with gusto and only gained muscle.

He felt her looking at him and wondered if he'd gotten sauce on his chin.

"What?"

"Why did you get into this line of work?" There

was a smudge of cheese on his face. Taking another napkin from the holder, she brushed it against his cheek.

Sam could have sworn he felt her fingers through the paper.

Setting the slice down, he rolled her question over in his mind. The choice wasn't something he had thought long and hard about. It was just something that had evolved. By the time he'd made his move to the agency, it had felt right.

But she was waiting, so he framed the best answer he could.

"I think kids have a right to enjoy innocence for as long as possible. It fades fast enough without having someone rip it away from you. I think of someone taking one of my nephews or my niece away from the parents who love them, the home they know— and a rage builds inside me. There's no excuse for it. None. People like that should be hauled out and shot. No appeal."

He blew out a breath, his words echoing in his head. She probably thought he was some sort of fanatic. He lowered his voice.

"The last case I worked on the police force was a kidnapping. A nine-month-old baby. Someone broke into the house and stole her while her grandmother was sleeping in the next room." He would remember the stricken look on that old woman's face until the day he died.

Savannah was almost afraid to ask. "Did you find the baby?"

He paused a moment, remembering. Remembering the small body, left for dead. Barely breathing. He'd cradled the tiny infant in his arms while his partner had driven like a madman to get her to the hospital in time. Even now, he felt a tightening in his chest.

"Yeah."

She had to ask the next question, even though there was something in his voice that made her afraid of what lay ahead.

"Alive?"

He looked at Savannah, realizing what had to be on her mind. He hadn't meant to mislead her. "Yes, she was alive. Just barely. We got her to the hospital in time. The kidnapper had gotten his ransom and then wanted to get rid of the inconvenient 'evidence.'"

It had taken three men to pull him off the criminal when they had finally tracked him down. Sam set his mouth hard. He'd come very close to murder that day. Closer than he ever wanted to be. It taught him things about himself, taught him that he always had to remain on his guard, even against himself.

"I guess I got a little too intense when we found him. I didn't like what I saw in myself." That was when he'd discovered that there was a darker side to everyone. Even him. "Neither did the captain. I thought it was better for everyone if I went my own way." He shrugged. He believed that he had more control now, that he could restrain himself if he were faced with the same situation again. At least, he wanted to think that. "Cade came into my life at the right time."

Savannah's eyebrows drew together as she tried to remember. "I thought you said Megan introduced you."

"She did. She'd worked on Cade's case when his son was kidnapped. She was with the FBI then." He smiled, recalling Megan's wording, and paraphrased it for Savannah's benefit: "But the Bureau was 'too confining' for her, so when Cade began ChildFinders, she quit the Bureau and came to work with him."

There was a softness in his face when he talked of the agency's only female partner. Questions rose in Savannah's mind. Questions that she really didn't have the right to ask. She asked anyway.

"Are you and Megan…?"

She couldn't find the word that she wanted to use. Anything she came up with would have given him the wrong impression.

Or maybe the right one.

Sam laughed, trying to picture himself with Megan. Petite, lively and feisty as hell, Megan was probably one of the most beautiful women he'd ever met, but there had never been any spark between them. And he figured it was better that way.

"We go back a long way, but Megan and I know too much about each other to get involved."

That didn't seem like a stumbling block to Savannah. If anything, it was the opposite. "I thought that was the basis of a good relationship—to know a lot about each other."

"Maybe." It occurred to him that he wanted to know more about Savannah. More than he'd already discovered by tapping into her personnel file on the computer. He'd meant to scroll past it, but found himself reading instead. Absorbing. "In this case, it's more like knowing a lot about your sister."

"She would make one beautiful sister."

There was no jealousy in her voice, he realized. Only admiration. Another woman would have been catty. But then, Savannah had no need to feel threatened by anyone. "Yes, she would."

He was looking at her strangely, and she couldn't read his expression. "What is it?"

He'd been struggling with his conscience and with his needs since they'd walked into the house. No, he corrected, since he'd woken up this morning. Right now, the forces of good were definitely not holding their own.

Leaning over, he ran his thumb along her lower lip. Torturing himself.

"I've wanted to kiss you all day."

If she listened, she could hear her heart pounding. There were no doubts now. Maybe they would come later, but for now, he was all that she wanted. All that she needed. If there were promises that hadn't been made, so be it. He was her comfort. And her fire. And she needed both.

"That's good," she said softly, "because I've needed to be kissed all day."

Once the words were out of her mouth, it unleashed

the flood of emotion she'd been trying to dam up. She stopped trying.

Savannah raised her face to his. "Kiss me, Sam. Make me forget all these terrible thoughts that are haunting me. Please," she breathed.

"Shhh." He cupped his hands around her face and felt his heart tighten, just as it had last night. "You should never have to ask for something like that." *Not when you make a man want to drop to his knees in reverence for being allowed to spend even a moment in your presence,* he added silently.

Sam kissed her then, tenderly pressing his lips to hers. Unprepared for the ardor he met. It was like testing the waters with his fingers only to have something grasp his wrist and pull him down into a whirlpool. A whirlpool that dragged him off for a wild ride through white-water rapids.

They were breathless immediately.

Breathless and wanting and eager.

Sam felt her straining against him, and he had to hold himself back to keep from ripping the clothes from her body. He couldn't begin to recognize himself or the emotions bouncing through him with such immeasurable energy.

This wasn't him.

There'd never been this frenzy seizing his body before. Bending it to its will.

He wasn't a womanizer, but there had been a fair number of women in his life. Women he'd enjoyed and who had enjoyed him.

But always, always, he'd been in possession of his

mind, of his thoughts. Now it seemed as if they were crashing and colliding, breaking up into fragments in the heat of his desire.

He couldn't seem to collect himself.

He didn't want to.

She was like water to his thirst, air to his oxygen-starved body. He felt entirely dependent on Savannah for his very life.

He didn't like being dependent, but he was too consumed by her to rebel. To even contemplate rebelling.

All he knew was that he needed her. Needed to feel her skin, soft and silken, beneath his fingers. Needed to feel the pulse in her throat throbbing against his lips as he pressed kiss after kiss there.

Needed, most of all, to feel born again in her burning desire for him.

All day, Savannah had felt as if she were sleep-walking through a never-ending nightmare. Only now did she feel alive—alive in the wake of Sam's touch, in the wake of his passionate kiss.

As he stripped away her clothing, and as she frantically stripped away his to feel his hard, naked body against hers, anticipation vibrated through every part of her. She wanted to make love with him. To him. And to have him make love not just with her but *to* her with all the wild, unbridled passion that there was between a man and a woman.

She wanted to feel…everything.

She never knew it could be like this, had never dreamed that it could be this passionate, this mind-numbing, this overwhelming.

Her need for him seemed bottomless, and even as she gloried in the sensations vibrating through her, her need frightened her. To need was to be vulnerable, and she'd been needy, been vulnerable. Been disappointed.

It was logical to be afraid.

But logic was something that couldn't find her here in this fiery, safe place Sam had created for her in his arms. Couldn't find her when her thoughts all turned to dandelion seeds being blown away in the wind. There was nothing left where logic could root.

Savannah groaned, only distantly aware that somehow they had wound up on the floor. Her heart pounding in her ears, she arched her body to capture every sweet sensation as his lips and tongue forged a trail along her skin. Her skin sizzled, dampened by his moisture, dried by his breath.

And then it was happening. He was taking her, making love to her with his hands, his mouth. Her body trembled as it sailed on the crest of another climax that he'd created for her.

And then another.

Everywhere he touched, the madness followed: the wave taking her up and over, but never quite down again. No matter how much she tried, Savannah couldn't catch her breath.

He made her head spin.

He made her want to give her heart again.

Sam had never met anyone remotely like her. So willing, so able. So incredibly supple and agile that he thought every part of her must be double-jointed.

Her boundless desire humbled him as it took him prisoner. And made him never want to break free.

Cradling her body beneath his, unable to hold himself back any longer, Sam linked his hands with hers. She opened her eyes then, and looked into his eyes. Looked into his soul. And captured it.

Her chest was heaving, rubbing against his. Urging him on.

Words he'd never said to any woman echoed in his brain, demanding release. But if he said them, then he could never take them back. And he wouldn't trap her this way. It wasn't fair. What she felt was need created out of the terrible moment in which she found herself. It wasn't because of any true feelings she had for him. But he could live with that, he told himself. And down the line he could make peace with it.

If he could have her now.

A sheen of sweat covered their bodies as he lowered himself into her. Her eyes didn't drift closed, instead they widened. Widened still more as he began to move.

Lifting her hips, molding herself to him, Savannah mimicked his rhythm.

The pace of their dance increased, growing faster and faster until it set a tempo of its own and he had to hurry to keep up.

He tasted her gasp in his mouth as she reached the summit a beat before he did. And then he was enveloped by it, by a sensation that, at that moment, he felt he could have died for.

And sharing it with the woman he knew he would have died for.

The thought remained echoing in his mind, lingering long after the euphoria had slipped back into the shadows again.

Sam held her close to him, while outside, twilight embraced the world.

Held her and loved her. And wished from the bottom of his soul that he didn't.

Chapter 14

Sam had learned that even with a gut instinct, you have to back off sometimes in order to allow it to gel. There was such a thing as trying too hard, and he knew that he was.

What had been bothering him about Elliott's family medical records gelled the next morning in Savannah's kitchen.

A desire for coffee and her—not in that order—had brought him downstairs. He'd woken up to find her side of the bed empty, and the sheets fairly cool. Instantly alert, Sam threw on his jeans, grabbed his shirt and padded down the stairs barefoot, looking for her. A feeling of unease shadowed him.

He found Savannah in the kitchen, crying.

Sitting on the stool closest to the wall, Savannah seemed to have physically withdrawn into herself.

Her body shook with sobs that she was trying—with some success—to muffle.

The sight of her, so distraught, shook him down to the core of his being. The helplessness that held him captive, rendering him unable to remedy the situation for her, only heightened his frustration.

Crossing to her, Sam whispered her name, afraid of startling her. "Savannah?"

She turned away from him, obviously not wanting Sam to see her so completely out of control. But he wouldn't leave the room, wouldn't leave her alone on this desolate island on which she found herself. Instead, though she tried to push him away when he came to her, Sam patiently gathered her into his arms and held her.

He stroked her hair, letting her cry against his chest. Feeling useless. All he could do was let her know that she wasn't alone. Because he loved her.

"I know. I know," he told her softly against her hair. "But we'll find her. You have to believe that, Savannah. We're going to find her."

After a moment, she raised her head. She looked up at him, knowing he was doing everything he possibly could.

Knowing also that it might not be good enough.

She gulped in air before she could speak. "I just…looked at the…calendar and then I just lost it."

She was pointing toward the wall. He didn't bother looking at the calendar that he knew hung there; he'd noted it before. It depicted a Norman Rockwell cover from the *Saturday Evening Post*.

"Is it her birthday?"

Savannah shook her head. "No, nothing like that. It's just that I—she had an appointment today…at 9 o'clock…just well-child care…I forgot… And now I won't be able to…" Her voice broke again.

The barely audible words struck a chord. Something flashed in his mind, momentarily illuminating everything. Pushing aside the sympathy he felt.

Sam grasped Savannah by her shoulders and held her away from him. Excitement throbbed through his veins. "What did you just say?"

Stunned by his reaction, she tried to think. "That I won't be able to—"

"No, no, before that." Agitated, he waved her sentence away. She'd said something to stimulate a thought, but he was losing it again. "Something about her appointment."

Savannah stared at him, not knowing what he wanted from her. "Her visit to the doctor?"

Those weren't the words she'd used. He needed the exact words. "You called it something."

Her mind jumbled, Savannah tried to sort out her words. "Well-child care?"

And then it just fell into place as if it had always been there. "That's it."

"What's it?" Wiping her tears away with the back of her hand, Savannah stared at him. He wasn't making any sense. "I don't understand. What are you talking about?"

"It's what's been bugging me about your friend

Elliott's medical files.'' Now that he thought about it, it seemed so clear. How could he not have seen it?

Now that he'd figured out what hadn't seemed right about Elliott's records, he wanted to get to the office to look at the file again as soon as possible. He needed to play this through.

''What are you—'' Savannah began.

''C'mon.'' One arm around Savannah, Sam picked up a piece of now-cold toast from the stack on the dish. It would have to serve as breakfast until later. This was more important. ''I want to get to the office to check this out.''

He still hadn't said anything to make what he was going on about any clearer, although his excitement was infectious. Despite the lack of foundation, she felt her hope strengthening.

''Check what out?''

''A hunch.'' But he had a good feeling about it— a very good feeling that it was going to be more than just a hunch.

She looked down at the floor. Sam was standing there in his bare feet. ''Don't you need your shoes?''

Glancing down, he realized he'd forgotten to put them on.

''Right.'' Sam laughed, kissing her. ''Always thinking.'' He raced up the stairs to get his shoes.

''I still don't understand what you're getting at,'' Savannah said as she walked into the office after Sam.

He went straight to the computer and turned it on, then drummed his fingers on the desk as he waited for the system to boot up and the monitor to begin flashing progress messages.

His sisters-in-law were always talking about having to cart one or another of the kids off to see the doctor for routine checkups. They said it was a good thing that the insurance companies covered well-child care with all its inoculations and tests, because those visits sometimes turned out to be more costly than visits for colds and ear infections.

Savannah was looking at him expectantly. It was time to stop hedging and let her in on it. "Most parents take their kids in for well-child care pretty regularly these days, right?"

"Right," she agreed slowly.

The system came on. Sam immediately began working his way through Big Bytes' personnel files until he came to Elliott's. Sam raised his eyes to Savannah. "Would you say that Elliott's a good father?"

Her own father should have been half as caring as Elliott was, she thought.

"A very good father. He and his wife dote on Emily. He says Emily's the light of both their lives." Standing behind Sam, she looked at the screen and saw nothing to have triggered his enthusiasm. What was he getting at? "Why?"

"Doting parents want to make sure their daughter's well, right?" Sam scrolled into Emily's file. It was just as he remembered. Sam pointed to the dates. "Where's the well-child care? There's nothing on Emily after February. We're halfway through August.'' He turned in his chair to face her. ''Where're the pediatrician bills?''

It didn't look right to her either, but there might be reasons for that. ''Perhaps they didn't bother sending them in?''

Sam shook his head. ''He picked the HMO option for his insurance.'' Sam pointed to the bottom of the screen where the legend was highlighted. ''The charges come in automatically.''

Puzzled, Savannah elbowed Sam out of the way and moved the keyboard closer to her. She went from screen to screen within the file, looking for claims. All the previous years were there. Emily saw her pediatrician, Dr. Sawyer, like clockwork. Except for this year.

Sam was right. She pushed the keyboard back to him, thinking.

''Wait a minute, maybe they're in the pending file for some reason.'' It seemed a likely guess to her. She'd gone round and round with the insurance company about one of Aimee's earlier claims because they insisted a diagnosis was missing, even though it had been included in the original billing. ''The adjusters hold things up when they need a piece of information. Maybe the charges are there.''

Moving the keyboard closer to her again, Savannah went to a different file within the program and opened it. There was a claim pending. Opening that, she discovered that the claim was for an ambulance ride on February sixteenth.

Sam read out loud the note attached to the file.

"'Ambulance service not affiliated with your current provider. Payment pending receipt of description of the nature of emergency, the emergency room bill and the attending physician statement.'" Sam looked at Savannah. "What was Emily in the emergency room for?"

It was all news to Savannah. "I didn't know Emily went to the hospital."

This had to mean something—although he wasn't sure just what yet. "I thought you said you and Elliott were close."

"We are," she protested. "That is, I thought…" Savannah no longer knew what to think. She saw Sam pick up the telephone receiver. "Who are you calling?"

"The ambulance service." He read the number off the claim form. It was a private company, not associated with any local hospital. That probably made it easier, he thought. "They have to have records."

"But we can't disclose that information," the woman on the other end told him.

Savannah listened in fascination as Sam's voice took on a definite Brooklyn tone.

"Sure you can," he insisted irritably. "Look, I'm with Casualty Life Insurance, and we're trying to figure out our liability in this case. The claimant's the girl's father, and he's suing the company for millions, saying this whole thing was our fault."

The woman on the other end sounded puzzled.

"How is it your fault his daughter drowned in his pool?"

Sam froze. "She drowned?"

"Says right here in the paramedics' report that the little girl was D.O.A. Are you sure you're calling about the right case?" Suspicion entered the woman's voice. "What did you say your name was?"

Sam hung up without answering. He'd heard enough. "When did you last see Emily?" he asked Savannah.

Savannah tried to think. She was tempted to say Easter, but remembered that Elliott and his family hadn't attended the company party.

"Christmas." She hadn't realized that it had been that long. "The last couple of company gatherings, Elliott said Emily wasn't feeling well, and his wife didn't want to take a chance on her getting sick." The excuses began to link together in her mind. Elliott had canceled their joint family vacation because he said Claire was sick.

Savannah began to feel ill.

"I'd say it was a little late for that," Sam pronounced.

Savannah couldn't believe it. How could Emily be dead, and Elliott not have said anything about it to her? To anyone? "Sam, there has to be some mistake."

"If there is, we may be the ones who made it." He should have gone with his instincts and pressed Elliott harder, sooner.

A sense of urgency filled him. He got up without

bothering to shut down the computer. He caught Savannah's hand and hurried for the door. "We're going to Elliott's home, and I'm phoning Underwood to have him meet us there. I think Elliott has Aimee."

With Savannah directing him to Elliott's Lake Forest home, Sam flew down the San Joaquin Toll Road. He knew the image of his whizzing car was being captured by the cameras that were set up every few miles along the new route. He figured there would be a whole raft of tickets coming his way in the mail soon.

He'd deal with that later. The important thing was to make it to Elliott's house. Who knew how long it would be before the man disappeared for good? Elliott surely knew that it was only a matter of time before the net closed in around him. The man wasn't stupid.

Beside him, Savannah was still in a state of shock. Her best friend had taken her daughter. It just didn't seem real.

"How could it be Elliott?" she cried.

The answer was all too common. "You don't always know the people you're dealing with."

Taking the off-ramp, Sam made a sharp, fast right at the end. "You said he doted on Emily. Maybe her death sent him over the top. The very fact that he didn't talk about it to anyone shows that something wasn't right." He glanced at Savannah. "He's obviously not the stable man everyone thought he was."

"But I should have known," Savannah said harshly. "I should have known."

"Why?" Sam demanded as he took another turn, this one into the tree-lined development. "Because you can read minds?"

"No," she snapped, angry at herself for being so blind. "Because he was my friend."

The label hardly fit anymore. "Friends don't kidnap friends' children."

Remembering the address Savannah had given him, he read the names on the street signs and turned down the right block. Elliott's house was located in the middle. Sam saw the man walking out the front door. They weren't too late.

He brought the car to a screeching halt. "Looks like our friend is planning on going somewhere."

Elliott, a suitcase in each hand, was rushing from the house to the gray car parked in the driveway. He looked completely oblivious to everything but what he was doing. Even from where they were, Savannah could see that he was unusually nervous.

Disbelief warred with outrage. Outrage won. Savannah was out of the car before Sam could stop her.

He'd raced here to stop Elliott from leaving, but he would have preferred waiting for Underwood first. The arrest had to be by the rules. Savannah just took that away from him. Jumping out of the car, he hurried after her.

"Savannah, no, wait for Underwood."

But she'd spent the last endless week waiting. She wasn't going to wait another second.

"How could you?" she demanded, confronting Elliott. "How could you do this to me?"

Elliott had just thrown the second suitcase into the trunk. He jerked his head up at the sound of Savannah's voice, narrowly avoiding hitting his head on the raised hood. The guilt written across his face made denial futile.

There was panic in his voice. "Savannah, what are you doing here?"

How dare he still pretend? "I've come for her, Elliott. I've come for my daughter. Where is she? Is she in the house?"

Without waiting for him to answer, Savannah spun on her heel and ran up the walk to the house.

Elliott nearly tripped over the rock border around his wife's neglected garden as he jockeyed for position ahead of Savannah. Completely ignoring Sam, Elliott attempted to block Savannah's entry.

"No, please, Savannah, you can't go in there."

"Why not?" she demanded. "Because I'll find her? I can't understand how you could have done something so horrific, Elliott. How could you steal Aimee away and then stand there, pretending to be my friend, pretending to be sympathetic? I *trusted* you," she spat.

Enraged, she grasped the man's arm to shove him out of her way.

Elliott's eyes moved frantically from Savannah's face to Sam's and then back again. He stumbled backward, still trying to bar her way, even though he knew it was useless. They were almost inside.

"I *am* your friend," he insisted, "and I was sorry—*am* sorry," he stuttered, "but you have to understand—"

Sam had had about all he could stand. "Understand what?" he demanded, his voice low and terrifyingly steely. "That you'd traded on your friendship and stole Savannah's daughter to take your own daughter's place?"

Elliott's jaw slackened as realization seemed to set in. "You know about Emily?"

Savannah didn't answer. Shoving Elliott aside, she threw open the front door and hurried inside. She looked around frantically. With the curtains all drawn, the rooms were bathed in darkness.

"Aimee, where are you? Aimee," she called, "it's Mommy. Where are you, baby?"

"Then you have to know about Claire," Elliott was babbling, following her. "You have to know how this has affected her. I begged her to see a doctor, to get help, but all she'd do was ask me to help her find Emily. That she'd lost Emily and had to find her." His voice broke; he was sobbing now. "When I came home and found her dressing Aimee in Emily's clothes, I didn't know what to do."

Sam caught the man by the arm and jerked Elliott around to face him.

"*She* took Aimee?" he demanded.

Looking stricken and sick, Elliott nodded. More tears gathered in his eyes.

"I know I should have taken her back right away, but Claire—Claire's mind is so fragile now. I didn't want to lose her, too." Breaking away from Sam, he tried to get Savannah's attention, to get her forgiveness. "I just couldn't lose them both."

But she had no sympathy for him, not now. Not when she still hadn't found her daughter. Frantically, Savannah went from one room to another, searching.

"Aimee!"

She found her daughter in Emily's old room, clutched in Claire's arms. Sitting in a rocking chair, Claire held Aimee tightly to her. She was rocking back and forth. The other woman, her hair disheveled, her eyes glassy, seemed oblivious to anyone but the little girl she held on her lap.

"Now, don't squirm, Emily. I have to dress you. We're going on a long trip, and I want you to look pretty. You can look pretty for Momma, can't you, honey?"

Empathy twined with relief, and edged out anger. Savannah's heart twisted in her chest at the sight of Claire talking, not to Aimee, but to the memory of her dead child.

And then Aimee saw Savannah, and jumped from Claire's lap. Claire cried out and tried to catch her arm, but Aimee dove for the protection of her mother's arms.

On her knees, trying not to sob, Savannah opened her arms to her daughter and enveloped her small body, pressing it close to hers.

Thank you, God.

"Mommy, Mommy," Aimee cried, "you're

squishing me." The words were muffled against Savannah's chest. "Where were you?"

"Looking for you, baby, looking for you." Stroking Aimee's hair, Savannah forced the words out through a throat that was tightening. "But it's over now. All over. I'm here, and I'm never letting you out of my sight as long as I live." Rising to her feet, she held on to Aimee as Sam ushered them both from the room.

"C'mon." Sam pushed past an impotent Elliott, knowing the man wasn't going to try to stop them anymore. "Let's get you out of here."

The wail of sirens mingled with the cries of Claire, calling for Emily to come back.

Chapter 15

Somehow, someone listening to the police radio had alerted the media about Aimee's discovery.

By the time Sam and Savannah arrived on her block with Aimee tucked safely in her car seat in the back, there were reporters camped all over Savannah's lawn. People were milling around, and vehicles with news logos pasted on their sides parked along every available stretch of curb for three blocks.

It looked like a circus waiting to happen.

Sam slowed the car. He had half a minute, maybe less, before someone recognized them, and the media began swarming.

"Maybe I'd better take you two to my place," he suggested.

Sitting in the back with Aimee, Savannah turned down the offer.

"No, I want to bring Aimee home."

She felt that it was important to the little girl's mental well-being to be in familiar surroundings as quickly as possible. No one was going to chase either of them away from their home.

That wouldn't have been Sam's choice, but he didn't argue with her. Instead, he edged the car onto Savannah's driveway as the crowd parted just enough for him to park. Getting out first, he ran interference for Savannah and Aimee up to the front door.

He meant to hurry her inside, but Savannah, with Aimee in her arms, purposely stopped at the entrance. Cameras flashed and mikes were angled toward her face, as she gave a brief statement, thanking everyone for anything they might have done in connection with finding her daughter.

Sam waited until she was finished. "Okay, ladies and gentlemen, the show's over. Give them some breathing space."

"What's your part in this?" someone shouted over the din of voices.

"I'm the chauffeur," he answered flippantly, using his body to block any further access to either Savannah or her daughter. "Get inside," he ordered tersely, all but pushing Savannah into the house once she had the door opened.

Behind them, reporters, waiting to submerge Savannah in an endless sea of questions, protested the separation from this portion of the five-o'clock news. Protests and questions fell on deaf ears as Sam closed the door firmly in their faces.

Savannah looked relieved to have gotten in safely.

"I'll wait this out with you," he promised her, flipping the lock closed. Sam went to the window and drew the drapes. He knew that she didn't want to be left alone just yet.

That, he thought, would come later.

Looking over her shoulder, Savannah gave him a grateful smile. Still holding Aimee in her arms, she picked up the telephone and called her parents.

The ordeal was over.

The last of the reporters finally broke camp a little more than two hours later. Someone had received a hot tip on a new breaking story involving a shootout on the Riverside Freeway. The media was off and running.

Checking out the terrain, Sam moved back the drape and looked up and down the street. Everything seemed back to normal.

Whatever that was, he thought.

He heard her entering the living room behind him, and let the curtain fall back into place.

"They're gone," he announced.

Savannah nodded, dropping onto the sofa. It didn't occur to her until just this moment how truly exhausted she felt.

"Aimee just fell asleep," she told him. "She wanted to know why 'Aunt Claire' kept calling her Emily." Savannah blew out a long breath. "Thank God, she wasn't afraid, just confused. She told me she kept asking why they wouldn't let her go outside to play." Her mouth curved, but it wasn't a smile. "They told her there were bad people outside and they didn't want anything happening to her."

"There's irony for you," he commented. "The bad people were inside."

Leaning her head back against the cushion, she closed her eyes. She was still unable to fully absorb the fact that it was finally over. That Aimee was finally back where she belonged. Safe.

Thanks to Sam.

There was a great deal she had to thank him for. Savannah opened her eyes and looked at him. She'd half expected Sam to sit down beside her, but he remained standing by the window. He seemed so pensive, so distant. She wondered if that was just his way of unwinding. God knew, he'd earned the right to unwind.

She watched him, a vague feeling sneaking up on her that something was wrong. Maybe she was just imagining things. She was tired.

"I can't believe that it was Claire all along. That she'd been following me for the last few weeks, just waiting for a chance." Savannah shivered at the very thought. "And then, when I went shopping with Aimee in that crowded department store, she finally saw her opportunity. Aimee didn't think anything of it when Claire motioned her over. She thought she was taking her to see Emily." She forced back her tears again. "Poor Emily," she whispered. "I haven't told Aimee about her yet. She thinks that Emily's away on some vacation, like we went on earlier." Savannah looked up at him. "I would never have suspected Claire," she confessed, a trace of lingering bewilderment still evident in her voice.

He'd learned long ago to suspect everyone. That's what made him good at investigations and lousy at relationships, he supposed.

Restless, Sam shoved his hands into his pockets. "Elliott's being very cooperative with the police now that everything's out in the open." He'd checked in earlier with Underwood to make sure the detective didn't have any further need of him after he'd given his statement. "He almost looked relieved. He only broke down when he talked about Emily drowning in their swimming pool just after Valentine's Day."

Savannah shivered, envisioning it. "Just like in Eliza's vision," she murmured, realization dawning.

Eliza's vision had been of a little blond girl drowning. Emily had been blond. From a distance, Emily and Aimee had looked very much alike. Savannah closed her eyes for a moment.

There but for the grace of God...

Watching her, Sam was tempted to put his arms around Savannah. Control made him remain where he was. Touching her would only make this harder.

"Right vision, wrong kid," Sam agreed. "And it was a pool, not a lake." He shrugged. Maybe there was something to this psychic business after all. But that was unimportant. The only thing that mattered was that Aimee had been found.

Funny, he thought, how some people crumpled under adversity, while others shone. Elliott had crumpled. Calling in favors, Sam had been allowed to attend the police interview. Sam shared the details with Savannah; he knew that she'd want to hear.

"Elliott said that Claire was supposed to be watching Emily, but she went inside to get something to drink and when she came out again, Emily had fallen into the pool. According to Elliott, Claire couldn't live with the guilt, and her mind snapped. He didn't say anything to anyone because he was too overcome himself. He had a hard time living with it."

"Poor Elliott." Now that it was all over, she couldn't help feeling sorry for him. For both of them, really. She looked up at Sam. "What's going to happen to them?"

"Claire's probably going to a mental institution, at least for a while." That much, he knew, was a safe bet. "As for Elliott, that depends on the judge and jury, I guess."

She paused for a moment, looking down at her hands. "He'll need character witnesses."

The depth of her charity amazed him. "You'd do that?" Another woman would have wanted to see the kidnappers drawn and quartered.

Slowly, she nodded. "I can't forgive Elliott for what he put me through—but I can understand his desperation. His child, whom he adored, died. And his wife, whom he worshipped, went off the deep end. The man was trying to hold together the fragments of his life."

Sam shook his head. He thought he knew Savannah, but she continued to be a revelation. "You're something else, you know that?"

She shrugged off the compliment. She hadn't shared her feelings with Sam so that he would think she was doing something special. "I can't judge until I've been there."

Who had more of a right to judge? "You have, actually—in a way," he pointed out. "Someone took Aimee. You didn't react by stealing other people's children."

It was far more complex than that. "I was lucky. I had someone to help me."

She looked at him meaningfully. She'd been fortunate to have him come into her life just when she needed someone like him. Very fortunate.

Sam reminded himself that he was just someone who had helped her. He had to remember that and keep things in perspective. Whatever she felt for him was born of that sentiment. That gratitude. And as gratitude faded to find its proper place in her life, so would the feelings she thought she had for him.

Until they faded away, too.

He wanted to leave before he saw that light fade from her eyes. The light that now seemed to burn only for him. Sam didn't think he could bear watching it leave.

It was over and he knew it.

He'd done the job he was hired to do. All that remained was to tie up a few miscellaneous loose ends, and say goodbye.

All.

He hadn't realized, when she walked into his office an eternity ago, how hard this was going to be. But then, he hadn't known that she would awaken within him the man he could be. The man he had felt he had surrendered the right to be. Normal. Loving. In love.

Hell, he thought, struggling to keep his composure, this was going to be downright painful. Worse than the time he'd taken a bullet to the shoulder. At least you knew you'd heal from that.

He wasn't altogether sure about healing from this.

He looked toward the door. It was time. If he didn't go now, he didn't think he could go at all.

Savannah saw him make a move toward the front door. The reporters were finally gone. Aimee was asleep. They were alone. Why wasn't he holding her?

She rose to her feet. "You're leaving?"

"Yes."

She didn't like the way the word sounded. So final. A nervousness began to creep through her.

"But you'll be back." She waited for his assurance. Maybe there was something he had to see to, something that took him away from her now, but not for long.

A self-deprecating smile curved his mouth. "If the check to the agency bounces."

The flip remark was one she wasn't prepared for. Rising, Savannah looked at him incredulously as she crossed to him.

"And that's the only reason?"

He tried very hard to divorce himself from the words, from the feelings. He couldn't even achieve a worthy separation. "Savannah, my job was to find Aimee. I found Aimee. The job's over."

Something inside her, so newly rebuilt, was crumbling. "Is everything over?" Her voice was low, emotionless.

As gently as he could, he tried to make her understand. "There was no 'everything.' We were caught up in something, in the moment." *And I was caught up in the look in your eyes, in that half smile of yours.* He saw her eyes go flat. It was already beginning. "The moment's gone."

It cost her to bare her soul to him, but if that was the price to keep what they had, then she would pay it. "Maybe you were caught up in the moment, but I—"

He wouldn't let her say it, only to regret it later. He couldn't do that to her. "It's over, Savannah."

"Over?" she echoed, stunned, angry. "What's over? The way I feel isn't over. The kind of man you are isn't over. Don't drive wedges between us because you have some misconception about the kind of work you do separating you from a normal life. That's just an excuse. You're the one who counts, not your lifestyle. You're a good man, Sam, with a good heart and a lot to offer—"

He cut her off. "What you felt was gratitude. Don't mistake it for something more."

Gratitude. And he'd taken pity on her and let her "show" her gratitude by allowing her to make love with him. Well, he could just take it all and shove it!

"I see." She struggled to hold on to her temper.

Her tears. "Well, I won't embarrass you any further."
Walking over to her purse on the coffee table, she
opened it and pulled out her checkbook. The sound
of the pen clicking to expose a point seemed to echo
in the silent room. "Do I make this out to you or the
agency?"

"The agency." This was too hard, he thought. Too
hard. "Savannah, if you need anything—"

She signed her name. "No, thank you. I'll manage
just fine from here. I did before. No need to spread
any more gratitude around." Savannah tore off the
check and held it out to him. "This is the sum that
was agreed on, wasn't it?"

Sam didn't bother looking at it. The expression on
her face twisted him into knots.

"Savannah, I—"

But he had shut her out, and now it was her turn
to do the same. She took a few steps back.

"If you'll excuse me, I'm very tired right now."

"Sure." It was better this way. No painful small
talk, just take the check and go. He pocketed the piece
of paper. "Sure thing."

Sam let himself out.

It occurred to him, as he walked to his car, that
they hadn't said goodbye.

Megan Andreini looked up from her computer
when she saw Sam pass by her door. She'd been out
of the office for almost a week, working on a case,
and had read all about Aimee King's reunion with her
mother. It made her proud.

"Way to go, Sam!" she called out.

"Thanks."

Megan left her computer downloading a program, and walked into Sam's office. The look on his face was enough to send thunderclouds into hiding.

"You certainly don't look like a man who's just kept our good name and reputation alive," she commented.

Sam had come into the office because he'd run out of "vacation" time to take, and because he couldn't seem to find a place for himself in his own world anymore. Sam had tried to get on with his life. But everywhere he went, every step he took, she was there. In his mind. Haunting him like a perpetual beat that refused to fade away no matter what other sounds surrounded it or tried to drown it out.

She was the first thing he thought about in the morning, when he woke up and his mind was unguarded. She was the last thing he thought about at night, when he finally faded into an exhausted sleep.

She wouldn't let him alone.

Maybe work would make him feel human again. "I've got a lot on my mind, all right?"

Megan pretended to back away. "The thud you just heard was the head you just bit off falling on the floor. Your mind, huh?" She peered at his face. She'd never seen him look so dark before. "Sure that's the right body part?"

He didn't care to be probed. "You're beginning to sound more like a guy every day." Sam dropped the papers he was going through. What the hell was he looking for, anyway? He couldn't remember.

Megan grinned. "I take it you don't mean that in a good way." Growing serious, she got into his face. "Talk to me. What's wrong?"

He wasn't about to bare his soul to anyone. This would pass. He would just have to wait it out. If he lived that long.

"Nothing. Back off." He turned his back on her.

"All right, I will," she agreed. "At least until I can get a whip and a chair issued to protect myself." She shook her head. "Your mood is foul, Sammy. Careful or I'll tell Momma on you."

He raised his eyes to look at her. "Megan?"

"Yeah?" The question was innocently tendered.

"Go soak your head."

She nodded, pretending to accept his words of wisdom. "And my advice to you is, go see her."

The look in his eyes was positively dangerous. "I don't know who you're talking about."

With a sigh, Megan gave up. For now.

After two weeks of listening to growled answers and bitten-off sentences, Cade decided to take the matter into his own hands.

He walked into Sam's office and closed the door.

"You know, Sam, we're not zoned for bear. Especially not wounded bear. So we might have to drop you from the agency."

Sam looked at him. "What the hell are you talking about?"

"You." Cade came around his side of the desk. "Since you solved the Aimee King kidnapping, you've been hanging around here, contributing minimally and acting like a damn wounded bear. Now, are you going to go and see the woman? Or do I have to take you there myself and put the words into your mouth?"

Sam laughed shortly. "I'd like to see that—being that most of the time you're as animated and articulate as a tree."

Cade wasn't going to allow him to sidestep the issue. "We're talking about you, not me. And the future sanity of the people who work alongside of you," he added. Cade paused, waiting. Sam remained seated. "Get out of the office, Sam. I can't make it any plainer than that."

Muttering something under his breath, Sam rose to his feet and left.

It amazed Savannah that she could feel so happy and so unhappy at the same time. She treated each day with Aimee as if she'd been given a precious gift—a gift she knew she would never again take for granted.

But within each day there was an emptiness that was entirely new to her, an emptiness she didn't know how to fill. An emptiness that had Sam Walters written across it.

She would never have expected that she could become so attached in such an incredibly short amount of time. That she could miss someone so much. After all, what did she know about the man?

Enough to know she loved him.

You'd think, she scolded herself—depositing the final load of groceries from her car onto the kitchen counter—that she would have learned by now that men and she just didn't mix. Not on a permanent basis, at any rate.

But all lectures to the contrary, finding her way from one end of the day to the other was hell. If she hadn't had Aimee in her life, Savannah knew she would never have survived.

Dwelling on it wouldn't help. She had ice cream that was melting. Her parents were due to bring Aimee back in an hour, and she wanted to get things in order by then. Since Aimee's return, her parents had behaved like completely different people. Warm, loving. Classic grandparents.

It seemed there was hope for everything, she thought as she opened the refrigerator.

Or almost everything.

The doorbell rang. Savannah wondered if it was another reporter. After three weeks, for the most part, they had stopped calling, but that didn't mean she was in the clear yet.

The doorbell rang again. Maybe her parents were returning early. Putting the ice cream away, she hurried to the door, mentally bracing herself just in case it was a reporter.

But when she opened it, she was completely unprepared to find Sam standing there. Her heart leaped into her throat and refused to dislodge.

"Hi," he said stiffly. God, what was he going to say to her? How the hell was he going to bridge the gap he'd created with his own stupidity?

"Hi," she echoed back.

She wanted to hug him.

She wanted to beat on him until he was black and blue for putting her through hell.

Most of all, she wanted to touch him, to assure herself that he was real. It took a great deal of effort to keep her hands still.

She wasn't moving, he noted, wasn't opening the door any farther. Maybe this wasn't such a good idea. Still, he was here. He couldn't turn back. This was his only chance to make things right.

"Can I come in?"

Savannah hesitated a moment before finally stepping back. "Sure."

He looked just as good as ever, damn him. Maybe a little thinner. The way he ate, she would have thought that an impossibility.

She went back to unpacking her grocery bags.

"Something wrong with the check?" she asked sardonically.

Sam looked around, wondering where Aimee was. "What? Oh, no. It's fine," he said absently. He watched Savannah place cartons of milk in the refrigerator door. It looked like things were back to normal for her. Too bad he couldn't say the same for himself. "I just came by to see how you were doing."

She lifted a shoulder, let it drop, stalling to compose herself.

"Fine." She turned away as she stacked things in the pantry. "Finding our place in life again slowly. Aimee seems to have no negative effects at all. Elliott made sure she wasn't afraid, wasn't harmed. He kept telling her it was a game, and she seems to have believed him, thank God."

Savannah tossed bags of vegetables into the crisper without looking. It was an attempt to keep moving, keep busy, when what she really wanted to do was scream at him...

And throw her arms around his neck.

"I've gone to see him in prison. He's really very sorry..." She didn't want to talk about Elliott, not with Sam standing so close. "So, how are you doing?"

"Me?" His mouth curved a little, but his eyes weren't smiling. "I'm doing lousy."

"Oh." Savannah turned around. She hadn't expected him to say something like that. She didn't know what to feel. "I'm sorry to hear that."

The formality stuck in her throat, but she had no other options open to her. Not without breaching any of the hastily reconstructed walls she'd thrown up for herself. Acting uninterested, she went back to redistributing her groceries.

"Any particular reason?"

"Yeah. There's a particular reason, all right." Sam got in between Savannah and the counter, forcing her to stop unpacking and really look at him. "Seems everyone knows it but me. Cade threatened to throw me out of the agency because the building's not zoned for bears.''

'She stared, uncomprehending. ''Bears?''

''Yeah. Bears,'' he repeated. ''According to Cade and Megan, I've been behaving like a wounded one.''

She tossed her head, sending her hair flying over her shoulder.

''Gee, I thought the only animal you imitated was an ass.'' She couldn't help the smile that crept out.

He grinned then, feeling a little better. A little hopeful. ''I seem to be widening my repertoire.''

She stopped pretending to pay only marginal attention and looked up at him. She grew serious again. ''And what is it you want from me, Sam?''

Here it was. All or nothing, he thought. ''Everything. You.''

She waited, but he said nothing more. ''Are you planning on getting any more articulate than that?''

He could talk the ears off a brass monkey if he wanted to, but words about his own feelings had never come easily to him. Now was no different.

He stalled. ''Cade volunteered to come here and put words in my mouth, but it's not as if he has a whole lot to spare. Compared to him, the Sphinx is talkative. So I guess I'm going to have to do this on my own.''

This time, Savannah's smile was encouraging. ''I guess so.''

He took a deep breath. And Savannah into his

arms. Sam couldn't help thinking that she felt so right there.

"I miss you, Savannah. I've been trying not to, but I miss you. I miss hearing your voice, seeing your face, touching your skin. Maybe I lost the right to say this, but I—I…"

This was a man who put his life on the line every day, and he was stumbling over a simple phrase. She thought he was adorable. "You didn't lose any rights, Sam. Spit it out."

"I am, don't rush me."

"Rush you?" Her eyes widened. Did he have any idea what she'd been going through? "I've been waiting three long endless weeks for you."

Sam stopped struggling with his tongue and stared at her. "Waiting? Then you knew I'd be back?"

"I didn't know." That was just the trouble. She hadn't. If she had, then she wouldn't have felt so awful. "I just—hoped. Now you were saying…"

Sam looked into her eyes, and suddenly, it was easy. "I love you."

Warmth spiraled through her. Savannah threaded her arms around his neck—just the way she'd wanted to since he walked in.

"There, was that so tough?"

"No. I love you," he repeated.

Savannah grinned. "By George, he's got it."

"No, but I'd like to. And I'd like to have you— and Aimee—as well."

Her heart suddenly went very still. He couldn't mean… "What are you saying?"

"That I love you, and I want to marry you." He knew now that what she'd said before was true—about his life-style only being an excuse. What counted was that he did love them and that he wanted to make them happy. And would always strive to do that until his dying breath.

Savannah's heart resumed beating. It was going to be all right. "Boy, when you get the hang of something, you really get the hang of it, don't you?"

"Is that a stall?" he asked suspiciously.

"No, that's a 'yes.'" On her toes, she wound her arms around him more tightly. Her eyes held his. Just as his heart held hers. "It's been 'yes' since the first time you kissed me."

He brought his lips to hers and kissed her. "That long ago, huh?"

"Yes, that long ago." She kissed him back. "Not everyone's as slow as you."

"Maybe." The one he returned was longer still. "But I'm learning." He kissed her again. "Teach me some more."

Yes, she thought, kissing him back, he certainly was learning. And she had a feeling that she was going to have a hard time keeping up. But she was determined to die trying.

She smiled up into his eyes as warmth enveloped her. "You're my hero, you know. My hero for all seasons."

He wanted to be all things to her. This was certainly a start. "That's a tall order." He brushed his lips against hers again, the intensity continuing to grow. "I'd better get started filling it."

"You already have," she whispered, just before he took her breath away.

* * * * *

Don't miss Megan's romance,
A FOREVER KIND OF HERO,
coming only to Silhouette Intimate Moments
in August.

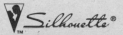

If you enjoyed what you just read,
then we've got an offer you can't resist!

Take 2 bestselling
love stories FREE!
Plus get a FREE surprise gift!

Coming in June 1999 from

Silhouette® Books...

Those matchmaking folks at Gulliver's Travels are at it again—and look who they're working their magic on this time, in

HOLIDAY Honeymoons

Two Tickets to Paradise

For the first time anywhere, enjoy these two new complete stories in one sizzling volume!

HIS FIRST FATHER'S DAY   **Merline Lovelace**
A little girl's search for her father leads her to Tony Peretti's front door...and leads *Tony* into the arms of his long-lost love—the child's mother!

MARRIED ON THE FOURTH   **Carole Buck**
Can summer love turn into the real thing? When it comes to Maddy Malone and Evan Blake's Independence Day romance, the answer is a definite "yes!"

Don't miss this brand-new release—
HOLIDAY HONEYMOONS: Two Tickets to Paradise—
coming June 1999, only from Silhouette Books.

Available at your favorite retail outlet.

Silhouette®

This August 1999, the legend
continues in Jacobsville

DIANA PALMER

LOVE WITH A
LONG, TALL TEXAN

A trio of brand-new short stories featuring
three irresistible Long, Tall Texans

GUY FENTON, LUKE CRAIG
and CHRISTOPHER DEVERELL...

This August 1999, Silhouette brings readers an
extra-special collection for Diana Palmer's legions
of fans. Diana spins three unforgettable stories of
love—Texas-style! Featuring the men you can't get
enough of from the wonderful town of Jacobsville,
this collection is a treasure for all fans!

They grow 'em tall in the saddle in Jacobsville—and
they're the best-looking, sweetest-talking men to be
found in the entire Lone Star state. They are proud,
hardworking men of steel and it will take
the perfect woman to melt their hearts!

**Don't miss this collection of original
Long, Tall Texans stories...available in
August 1999 at your favorite retail outlet.**

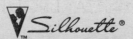

THE MACGREGORS OF OLD...

#1 *New York Times* bestselling author

NORA ROBERTS

has won readers' hearts with her enormously popular
MacGregor family saga. Now read about the MacGregors'
proud and passionate Scottish forebears in this
romantic, tempestuous tale set against the bloody
background of the historic battle of Culloden.

Coming in July 1999

REBELLION

One look at the ravishing red-haired beauty and Brigham
Langston was captivated. But though Serena MacGregor
had the face of an angel, she was a wildcat who spurned
his advances with a rapier-sharp tongue. To hot-tempered
Serena, Brigham was just another Englishman to be
despised. But in the arms of the dashing and dangerous
English lord, the proud Scottish beauty felt her hatred
melting with the heat of their passion.

Available at your favorite retail outlet.

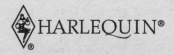

HARLEQUIN®

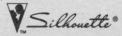